"No tale is quite so romantic as that of two lovers who have found each other again after a past lifetime of love. I recognized Lois as my soulmate the moment I saw her. I was getting ready to load some cargo into the hold when I happened to glance toward the gangplank and see a family of five coming on board—husband, wife, two young boys, one little girl. When I saw that little girl, it was as if she was suddenly bathed in a bright, golden light—and I knew I had rediscovered my soulmate."

—Bix Carter

"It was incredible. He looked exactly as he had appeared in my dreams. I suddenly somehow knew his present-life name as well. It was Todd. My heart was beating so fast that I really thought I would faint."

—Maureen Connors

"With each passing year, Sherry and I more completely learn the truth about what my wife calls our 'holy union.' We feel we are a unit that was too long kept apart and has now been reunited. We are convinced that we were destined to find each other again, but we will be forever grateful for the divine agency that assisted us in our rediscovery—for if we had remained lost to one another, we know that we would have lived out the remainder of our lives searching, knowing that the other was out there somewhere."

—Brad Steiger

DESTINED TO LOVE

BRAD STEIGER

PINNACLE BOOKS
KENSINGTON PUBLISHING CORP.

PINNACLE BOOKS are published by

Kensington Publishing Corp.
850 Third Avenue
New York, NY 10022

Pinnacle and the P logo Reg. U.S. Pat. & TM Off.

First Printing: January, 1996

Printed in the United States of America

Table Of Contents

Introduction

Of all the seen and unseen forces that inspire men and women on Earth, none is so powerful as the energy of unconditional love that emanates from the very spiritual essence of the creator of the universe.

While the giving of love without the imposition of conditional requirements may be largely a divine ideal toward which we mortals strive while on the plane of material reality, many of us have been blessed with the benevolent energy of a shared love that was able to transform us from ordinary men and women into quite extraordinary human beings, suddenly endowed with powers previously beyond our greatest expectations. And it is when such mystical insight penetrates the mental fog too often engendered by the conflicts and strictures of contemporary society that many of us are able to see clearly that the love that we share with our most significant other has been destined to be by forces far beyond the parameters of our limited earthly knowledge. Indeed, some of us have even been given the awareness that our romantic relationship with our beloved has continued through many lifetimes.

In the book *Angels of Love,* I told true stories of men and women who were brought together by the heavenly agency of angelic beings. In this volume, *Destined to Love,* I relate the true accounts of lovers who were compelled to be with one another because of paranormal manifestations such as telepathy, clairvoyance, prophetic visions, out-of-body experiences, dreams, the resurfacing of past-life memories, and the intervention of spirits, angels, or entities from UFOs.

Perhaps as you read these fascinating and inspirational stories of love found or reclaimed you'll be able to determine if you and your beloved were "destined to love."

Brad Steiger
September 1995

One

Sherry: My Destiny from the Stars

Sherry Hansen and I were married near the Sedona vortexes at midnight, August 17, 1987, during the Harmonic Convergence. Officiating at the private ceremony was my friend and spiritual brother the Rev. Jon Terrence Diegel. On September 30, we held another ceremony for our families, once again with the Rev. Diegel performing the service.

A few weeks before our marriage, Dr. Patricia Rochelle Diegel, Jon's wife, a psychologist-reincarnationist who has performed more than 45,000 past-life readings, told Sherry and me that we were not simply two entities coming together as one; we were equal parts of a whole being.

With each passing year, Sherry and I more completely learn the truth of Patricia's reading about what my beloved wife always calls our "holy union." We feel that we are a unit that was too long kept apart and has now been reunited.

In *Angels of Love,* I shared how we were literally brought back together by an angelic being that temporarily utilized the body of a stranger, and Sherry and I continue to feel the guidance and assistance of our heavenly guardians. We are convinced that we were destined to find each other again, but we will be forever grateful for the divine agency that assisted us in our rediscovery—for if we had remained lost to one another, we know we would have lived out the remainder of our lives searching, knowing always that the other was out there somewhere.

Once, during a deep, meditative experience, Sherry saw our spirits blending and exploding to form a new pyramid of living light and love. During our daily session of studying holy and inspired works together, we pray that we will always remain a living pyramid of mind, body, and spirit. We want to live in love and in light always. We pray that there is no power on Earth that will separate us, and we seek to hold fast in the power of Heaven that has blessed us.

The idea that certain men and women are destined to enter specific loving relationships may seem like a romantic conceit to the world-weary and the cynical, but Sherry and I are far from lone voices when we echo the words of the English poet Edward Robert Bulwer-Lytton: "We are but the instruments of heaven; our work is not design, but destiny." Or the thought of Goethe, who wrote, "Man supposes that he directs his life and governs his actions, when his existence is irretrievably under the control of destiny."

We are both eclectic in our beliefs. Sherry and I would never impose our thoughts, visions, or inspirations on anyone else. Our universalist approach to life will not suit everyone, and our openness to concepts and theories posed by those whom more orthodox thinkers might deem "too far out" has not always won us friends among those conservative-minded colleagues who caution us to espouse more comfortable positions. Our willingness to give every philosophical or religious expression a fair hearing before making any kind of assessment has brought us harsh criticism from those who argue that some folks' notions require immediate condemnation, lest one be tainted by "dangerous ideas."

With the understanding that I am writing about *our* truth and not necessarily *your* truth, I wish to present what I believe may offer a bit of additional evidence to our belief in our destined love.

In the mid-1960s, when she was a student, and then a staff member at the Lutheran School of Theology in Chicago, Sherry Hansen began to read scripture with a new vision, even to the extent of seeing the interaction of angels in the Old and New Testaments of the Bible as possible evidence of the activities of extraterrestrial or multidimensional beings. Having been reared in a strict Evangelical United Brethren family, she was almost completely unfamiliar with the teachings of other religions. She knew little about metaphysical or Eastern concepts of spirituality.

Because of her eclectic mind and universal consciousness, Sherry was beginning to find denominationalism getting in the way of her knowing God. She found herself echoing the words of the yogi Paramahansa Yogananda: "Let me be Christian, Jew, Hindu, Buddhist, or Moslem. I care not what my religion or race or nationality be, so long as I win my way to Thee."

Sherry became an ordained minister, and in the mid-1970s, she reached a crisis point in her life. At the urging of a fellow female minister, Sherry purposefully went somewhere where she knew no one would know where or who she was. She chose Virginia Beach.

After a week of total relaxation and a great deal of sleep, Sherry felt revitalized. She was told about a prayer-healing group that met nearby, and so she joined them one evening.

After the service, Sherry decided to stay longer and meditate. Later, as she left, she overheard two women talking about a psychic reading that one had conducted for the other. Almost as if directed by an unseen force, Sherry inquired about the nature of the psychic-sensitive's consultations.

Ellen Andrews's loving, gentle manner and energy seemed trustworthy to Sherry's skeptical mind. Sherry's basic religious fundamentalism caused her to be extremely cautious and doubtful about participating in activities such as clairvoyant readings; but Ellen seemed so open and free of occult leanings that Sherry scheduled an appointment.

Although she admits that she nearly canceled her reading "a hundred times," Sherry was reassured when she learned that Ellen Andrews's consultations were part of a professional research

project with the Association for Documentation
and Enlightenment. Although the psychic would
be in an altered state of consciousness, a trance
state, she would be guided through the reading by
a medical doctor.

Since Sherry was visiting from out of state, Ellen Andrews knew nothing about her. She was
asked to provide her name, birthdate, and place
of birth. Sherry was astonished when the entranced psychic-sensitive began making specific
references to personal matters about which she
could not possibly have had any knowledge.

Sherry was really startled when Ellen said she
(Sherry) was not of this solar system, that she was
a stranger here, "with purposes half-remembered
and half-forgotten." Ellen continued:

> We see a time when this soul chose to enter
> the Earth plane, coming, as we have said,
> from beyond our solar system, from out of
> the area of Cassiopeia, and into a physical
> body. There have not been numbers . . . of
> incarnations, but relatively few, this being
> [Sherry's] sixth on the earth plane.
>
> Not awakened fully to the purpose for
> which the soul came in, [Sherry is] to assist
> those caught in matter to an orientation with
> their divine father. She brings with her those
> outer-space attunements with a peculiar type
> of technology, a peculiar type of religion,
> metaphysics, or understanding of the divine.
>
> Many things make her still a stranger here,
> unfamiliar with the physical, unfamiliar with
> the Earth . . . and feeling a lack of attune-

ment or basic understanding with those
around her. At this time [1974], there are
many now incarnating from other regions of
the universe for similar purpose. She will
find from this time on those around her who
have more understanding of her thoughts, of
her origins, of her attunement.

The reading continued with detailed information
about the changes in Sherry's thought patterns, as
well as her physical, psychic, and vibrational
changes. The content of the reading was so deeply
personal and on target that Sherry wept in gratitude at finally finding someone, some presence,
that understood her struggles. It was truly as if an
angel of God was reaching out and giving her
healing balm for the body, mind, soul, and heart.
   The channeled information also focused on dif-
ficulties with emotional relationships.

For there are very few—if ever, indeed, she
has encountered one—in a male polarity who
can understand the quality of her thought,
her feelings, and her attunement with other
places . . . she is indeed making a choice
within her mind as to whether she would accept what is at hand or project for one more
attuned to her, not quite making the type of
relationship which she desires, yet not knowing if a more satisfactory one may be
brought forth.
   She will be paired with another, for work
. . . travel . . . the attunement of consciousness . . . and spiritual teachings . . . being

a healer, the one she will ultimately attract to herself will also be a healer, a spiritual teacher, and one whose origins will be similar to her own.

What was to have been a relatively brief reading lasted over an hour—until Ellen Andrews fainted. When the sensitive regained consciousness, she announced, shaken, that the remainder of her readings for the week were to be canceled.

Months later, Sherry learned that hers had been the first reading at that research center that had revealed a person who had an origin in another solar system. The psychic-sensitive, unaccustomed to extraterrestrial energy, may have fainted simply from the power of alien vibrations communicated to and through her. Subsequently, others with outer-space origins were discovered by the research center and a support group entitled "The Star People" was organized.

It was a good thing, Sherry has since observed, that the reading mentioned that the timetable for certain happenings was left to the *free will* of all concerned, because it took almost ten years for her perfect partner to arrive.

In 1967, I began collecting data from men and women who claimed to have an awareness that their "soul essences" had come to Earth from other worlds. In 1968, I developed a questionnaire that enabled me to define these individuals with such associated physical characteristics as extra or transitional vertebrae, lower than normal body temperature and blood pressure, chronic sinusitis, and sensitivity to electricity.

One of the most consistent elements in the pattern profile of these people was their sense of urgency that "the time is now" to help Earth and their fellow planetary citizens. It was that sense of mission that seemed most to distinguish these strangers.

In 1973, I chose a Chippewa name for such individuals and began referring to these men and women as "Star People." I introduced the concept to a mass audience in my book *The Gods of Aquarius: UFOs and the Transformation of Man* in 1976, and in 1981, I wrote *The Star People.*

Sherry was seriously wondering if the forecast of her meeting her destined mate was ever going to materialize when a friend told her about *The Star People.* Although we had met briefly in 1982, when she'd stopped by my office on her way to Europe on business, neither of us suspected that in 1987 she would become my wife. I felt a shock of recognition when I met her, but also a helplessness to act on my inner spiritual awareness. But angelic beings have their ways to help destined lovers to each other.

We both wonder why it took so long for us to be reunited. We can only accept the wisdom of a higher intelligence that deemed it necessary for us to acquire certain lessons in Schoolhouse Earth that would enrich us as evolving spiritual entities.

For us, the important thing is that we are together in the precious hours of the *now* and that we are here to support one another on all levels of being as we seek to fulfill our mission of assisting others to acknowledge their full physical and mental potential as human beings and to recognize the divine promise of their spiritual heritage as children of the loving creator that empowers the universe.

Two

My Wife, My Best Friend

Although we've actually spent very little time together, I've always had a pleasant mental association with Raymond Buckland that I know has to extend far beyond his English gentleman's good manners, his sense of humor, and the pixie-like twinkle in his eyes. We have always kept in touch wherever our journeys have taken us.

Although we had had some correspondence after his move to America in 1962, I don't believe we actually met until late 1975, when we were both speakers at an event sponsored by Carl and Sandra Weschcke of Llewellyn Publications in Saint Paul, Minnesota. Ray is best known to the metaphysical world as the individual primarily responsible for the introduction of contemporary witchcraft into the United States. The author of *A Pocket Guide to the Supernatural, Buckland's Complete Book of Witchcraft,* and *Witchcraft from the Inside,* he also founded a new variation of the old religion Seax-Wicca, a more open and democratic expression, and became a leading spokesperson for It to the general public.

A *poshrat,* or half-blooded gypsy, the London-born Buckland left the Church of England around age twelve to explore Spiritualism and metaphysics. A veteran of the Royal Air Force, Ray was educated at King's College School in London and received a doctorate in anthropology from Brantridge Forest College, Sussex. His spiritual search led him to study witchcraft, and in 1964, he received initiation into the craft by Gerald Gardner's High Priestess, Lady Olwen.

When I mentioned in correspondence that I was writing a book about destined lovers, Ray replied that his wife, Tara, had known for many years exactly the type of man she would marry, the age difference between them, his profession, etc.—and it all added up to Ray Buckland.

Here is Ray's account of their destined love match:

> On the rebound, from a failed marriage, I married a charming young lady with whom I had very little in common. We stayed together for a number of years, but slowly drifted farther and farther apart.
>
> In addition to my writing, I did a certain amount of teaching and often traveled around the country, giving lectures and leading workshops. In February 1982 I was invited to give a weekend of workshops in Cleveland for the fledgling Association for Consciousness Exploration, then known as the Chameleon Club. As part of the package, and to

promote the workshops, ACE president Jeff Rosenbaum arranged for me to appear on the television talk show *The Morning Exchange,* hosted by Fred Griffith on WEWS-TV.

Tara Cochran had read some of my books and had even, a year or two prior to this, written a fan letter to me, though I did not remember that then. She and a friend heard that I was going to be on television and watched the show together.

"I fell in love with him, seeing him on screen," Tara later told a friend.

She did admit to me some months later that she wondered about the earring I wore. She was delighted to learn the only reason I wore one was due to my Romany heritage. (A gypsy boy is given two gold earrings. When he grows up and finds "the one woman of his life" he gives her the right earring, which she usually wears on a fine chain around her neck.)

Seeing the impact that I'd had on Tara, this friend admitted that she knew Jeff Rosenbaum, who was instrumental in bringing me to Cleveland, and told me he was hosting a welcoming party at his house that evening. She and Tara were determined to attend.

I had had a long, hard day, and I tried to relax at the party. No sooner did I manage to disentangle myself from one person than another would buttonhole me. They were all charming people, but I knew I had a very full weekend ahead of me and wanted a little time to myself.

Two young ladies arrived. One hailed Jeff and then introduced her friend Tara. In turn they were introduced to me. I was immediately attracted to Tara. She was slim and attractive, with long blonde hair. She was intelligent and had a good sense of humor. Somehow, we seemed to find ourselves sitting alone together, eagerly exchanging our life stories. Tara had recently broken up with her boyfriend and had sworn off men for "at least two years," she said. With my two failed marriages, I was definitely not looking for any new involvements.

Before we knew it, it was past midnight and people were leaving. Tara and I were still ensconced in a corner, oblivious to everything around us. Eventually Jeff came and broke into the talk. Finally Tara left, reluctantly, but promised to be at my workshops the following morning.

I had difficulty starting the first workshop because Tara didn't show up at the start and I just couldn't get her out of my mind. But she arrived, slipping in unobtrusively, noticed solely by me. I felt a glow of happiness as our eyes met. She had been unavoidably delayed and was as anxious to get there as I was to have her there.

The weekend went all too quickly, with Tara and me spending all our spare time together. On Monday morning she came to see me off at the airport.

We wrote to one another every single day and ran up astronomical telephone bills.

Whenever I had to fly across country to give
a lecture I would arrange to be routed
through Cleveland. For a Canadian booking,
I flew to Cleveland and then Tara and I
drove her car to Toronto and back. It was a
wonderful trip. We even made a point of
stopping overnight at Niagara Falls and buy-
ing tacky souvenirs, as though it were a honeymoon trip!

By September I was separated from my
wife and Tara had moved down to be with
me in Virginia. We rented a house outside
Charlottesville and started to plan what we
wanted to do with our lives. We married and
moved to San Diego in August. There we
lived happily for over eight years before
moving to Ohio.

Tara and I have been married for over
twelve years. We have only become closer
over those years. We are each other's best
friend. Even though we both work at home,
we never tire of each other's company, never
get on each other's nerves. Rather, we miss
one another tremendously anytime we do
have to be apart, no matter for how short a
time.

Over the years, Tara has developed into a
writer and a fine teacher in her own right.
She has told me that she had known from
her young teens just how old she would be
when she got married and exactly the sort
of person who would be her husband. She
knew he would be English, that there would
be a marked age difference (I am twenty-one

years older than she is), and that he would be a writer or artist.

We now live on a small Midwestern farm where we lavish love on a variety of animals (lambs, sheep, a goat, some chickens, and a variety of pet snakes) and spend innumerable hours walking in the woods. It seems it was destiny that we should find one another just when we each had almost given up all hope of happiness.

Three

Led by His Dreams to Love

Whenever I think of lovers who fulfilled their destiny through dreams, I remember a colorful individual I met at an awareness seminar I conducted in New York City in the fall of 1984. Dom Spicuzza was a robust Italian American who laughed easily and seemed satisfied with his life. Most of all, he was contented with his dream lover who came true.

As Dom tells the story, he had never been out of the Bronx when Uncle Sam shipped him to Vietnam in 1969.

"I went right from the old neighborhood to boot camp and on to Nam before I could even learn how to spell Vietcong," Dom said. "Half my buddies were draft protesters, hippies, and peaceniks who accused me of being a baby butcher and a warmonger—at the same time that the sergeants in basic training were trying to transform me into a killing machine."

Strangely enough, Dom said, the only thing that gave him any stability in those awful days of chaos and conflict was a repetitive dream of a pretty young woman who lived in an idyllic country setting.

"She looked like a milkmaid in a dairy commercial on television," he said. "Every time I dreamt of her, I would feel like the guy in that old country song yearning for the green, green grass of home. And yet *my* home was subways, crowded streets, and a crammed apartment with a widowed father and four brothers."

Although the teeming streets and concrete canyons may have comprised the physical reality of Dom Spicuzza's home in the Bronx, throughout his troubled adolescent years, he had been pacified by a dream of walking through a picturesque covered bridge on a bright spring day in a rural area.

"I would feel real peace and happiness as I strolled beside a creek," he said. "Eventually, I would come to an old stone farmhouse. I was always dimly aware of someone walking beside me, though I could never make out who it was. I would enter the home and find myself in a neat country kitchen where a young girl with light brown hair would be stirring something in a big bowl."

According to Dom, the girl would always look up at him with great love and warmth in her large green eyes. The best part of the dream came when she walked right into his outstretched arms.

"It was like we had known each other for years," he said. "In my dream I would always call her by name—though I could never seem to remember it when I awakened. We would hug each other and hold each other like we never wanted to let go."

The dream became a kind of talisman for Dom.

"It got me through some pretty rough times," he remembered. "As a kid, I was always kind of shy around girls, and I went through a really bad scene with blackheads and pimples. But whenever a girl avoided me or gave me the cold shoulder, it didn't hurt me quite as much as it could have as I knew that somewhere this fantastic dream girl was waiting for me."

After the adolescent blights had left him, Dom dated a number of different girls and even went steady for a while.

"But at the weirdest and sometimes most awkward moments, I would start daydreaming about that beautiful lady in her country kitchen who I knew was waiting for me somewhere."

While Dom was in Vietnam, he had a particularly memorable dream:

> I had been drinking way too much while on R & R with some buddies. There was a lot of dope being smoked in Nam. I stayed away from that scene, but I managed to get really bombed out of my skull on beer and bourbon. I was trying my best to sleep my way out of a hangover when I saw my country girl so clearly and so three dimensionally that I would have sworn on all things I deem holy that she was right there with me in that two-bit hotel.

Dom said that his dream girl was shaking her finger at him and glaring at him in disgust.

She really looked upset with me, and I actually heard her talking. I mean, her words rang in my head to the point of pain. "Listen, you big, dumb lug," she scolded me, "I'm not going to wait for you forever. And I won't wait at *all* if you behave in such a disgusting manner. Look at you! You look and smell like a pig! And what if you get drunk on patrol and the enemy soldiers kill you because of your carelessness?"

Dom swore that he'd clean up his act after the vivid visionary experience, and he made a determined effort to tone down his party-time rest and relaxation activities.

Through the unfathomable process of job assignments often associated with the military, Dom, who had barely known how to drive when he'd entered the service, found himself assigned to a motor pool.

"I think Pop had a car when we were kids, but who needs a car in the city? They're usually more trouble than they're worth," Dom explained.

"But Pop always brought us boys up to try to make the best of any situation, so I made up my mind to learn as much as possible about the mechanical aspects of the vehicles in my charge. I also focused on becoming a really good driver."

Upon his discharge in 1971, Dom got a job with a trucking firm that transported produce from the farming regions of upstate New York to the grocery stores in the Big Apple.

"I've since learned through reading metaphysical books and taking workshops like yours, Brad, that there are no coincidences in life," he said.

"But one day I got lost and found myself suddenly on a country road that started looking very familiar. Pretty soon I knew I recognized it from my dreams, and I knew that right around the next bend I would see the old covered bridge, the creek, and the stone farmhouse. And I started to pray that I would also see *her* in real life!"

Within the next few moments, Dom was truly seeing it all—exactly as he had in his dreams so many times before.

"There was the stone farmhouse right in front of me. All I had to do was to turn down the lane. I knew *she* was there, in that house, waiting for me!"

Or was she?

What if she had decided not to wait for him any longer and had gotten married to someone else?

He was twenty-four years old. He had been having those dreams of his country girl since he was eleven or twelve.

"I knew better than to just stride boldly into the kitchen, the way I did in my dreams," Dom said. "I didn't want to be arrested for breaking and entering . . . or to be shot by a protective father—or worse, a jealous husband. I prayed that I had not found her after all these years only to find her married to someone else."

When he pulled his truck into the graveled farmyard, Dom was surprised to see a man from the vegetable market come out of the farmhouse to investigate.

Dom knew the man only as "Hugh," and he didn't know if the farmer would even recognize him.

"Hey, Big City Boy," the farmer teased him. "You lost or something?"

Hugh was about his age, Dom reckoned, maybe a few years older. Was he his dream girl's husband?

Dom admitted that he was lost, then asked if he might use the farmer's telephone to call his boss and explain why he'd be late.

As Hugh walked beside him to the stone farmhouse, Dom remembered how in his dreams there had always been someone near him as he'd entered the home. Someone whose features he could never quite distinguish.

"I was so nervous that I could hardly breathe," Dom recalled. "In the next instant, I was inside the warm kitchen and I was staring at the back of a girl with light brown hair who was stirring something in a large mixing bowl. *Everything was just as it had been in all those dreams!*"

When the young woman turned to acknowledge the presence of a stranger in the house, Dom beheld the beautiful features of the girl of his dreams.

Suddenly, he remembered her name.

"Linda!" He nearly shouted his joy and amazement.

The large green eyes blinked, and the full red lips worked at a quizzical smile in a manner that had become familiar to Dom over the previous twelve years.

Hugh edged between them. His large fists had bunched, and the farmer didn't look nearly so hospitable as he had a few minutes before.

"How is it that you know my sister's name?"

Hugh wanted to know. "Have you ever met her before?"

"At the sound of the word 'sister,' a one-thousand-voice choir of angels sang a chorus of 'Hallelujah.'" Dom laughed at the memory. "If Hugh had said 'wife,' I probably would have gotten right back in my truck and driven it off the nearest cliff."

To answer Hugh's direct inquiry, Dom smiled and responded truthfully, "Only in my dreams."

When the young farmer frowned and narrowed his eyes, Dom said, "Linda means 'pretty' in Spanish. Your sister certainly is pretty, right? I guess it was just a coincidence that Linda is also her name."

Dom's open smile and his quick-witted compliment won him an invitation to dinner.

"That was all the opening I needed," Dom said. "After another visit to the farmstead, Linda accepted my invitation to dinner. After another couple of dates, I told her how she had been my dream girl for the past dozen years. She didn't laugh at me or think I was putting her on. I'll never forget the way she just kind of smiled knowingly when I told her about my dreams.

"Now I drive the truck from the country to the city, instead of the other way around," he said, concluding his account of his dream lover come true. "Linda and I have a small truck garden next to Hugh's farm. This countryside has the green, green grass of my true home, and it has the green, green eyes of my true love."

Four

Dreams of a Past-Life Lover

I had to ask Maureen Conners to repeat herself.

"I'm serious, Brad." The vivacious brunette laughed at my disbelief. "I first dreamed about the man who would be my husband in my present life when I was five or six years old. I swear it!"

"But you didn't actually *know* him when you were five or six years old?" I asked, wanting to get the jumble of facts as straight in my mind as possible.

"Oh, no." Maureen shook her head vigorously. "We didn't meet on the physical plane until we were in graduate school."

I had to pursue one last point for clarification. "But you knew that he had also been your husband in a past-life experience."

Maureen gave me an enthusiastic "thumbs up" and a broad smile of approval. "Now you've got it, Brad."

I had been conducting a workshop in past-life awareness in Scottsdale, Arizona, and during the dinner break, Maureen Conners had asked if she might join me to describe her unique situation, in which she had literally grown up with her past-life lover.

Maureen was a tall, slender woman in her late thirties with attractive streaks of gray in her dark hair. Quite dark-complexioned and tanned, she had brown eyes that seemed to glow with enthusiasm as she told me of her destined love match with her husband, Todd.

She began by telling me how, as a very young girl, she would always dream of the same place, a lovely cottage near a sandy stretch of beach.

"I'm certain that it must have been someplace on Cape Cod in Massachusetts," she said. "We visited the Cape a couple of summers ago. I feel that I could have found the exact area if we'd had more time."

The focal point of each dream, Maureen explained, was a blond-haired, blue-eyed man who she knew was her husband.

"And he was always standing before an easel, looking out toward the sea, painting something that had caught his attention in the magnificent expanse of ocean," she said. "From time to time, he would look away from the sea and smile at me with such love, such warmth, that I would be quite overcome with a terrible sense of longing."

I didn't mean to break the spell of her memory, but I had to chuckle over the intensity of such emotions. "Somewhat precocious for a six-year-old, wouldn't you say?"

Maureen nodded. She had taken no offense at my interruption. "I suppose such feelings *were* rather precocious. But, I can still feel the depth of those awful feelings of a lost love.

"When I was older and told my friends about my dreams, they would always start to laugh at this point. After all, I grew up in Kansas, far away from any ocean. And I have always been dark complexioned, with brown eyes. So the cynics have always gotten on my case about childish fantasies of a terrain and a mate that would be the opposite of my native environment and my general appearance."

As is the case with most people who profess past-life memories, Maureen had grown accustomed to the arguments of the skeptical mind. But the dreams of the man who she knew was her past-life husband persisted all through high school.

"I would dream about him at least once a month," she said. "Sometimes we would no longer be by the ocean, but in an apartment in some large city, probably New York, maybe Boston. Sometimes I would be posing for him in long, elegant dresses."

I asked Maureen how she appeared in these dreams.

"Quite different from my present-life appearance. I'm nearly five-ten in this life. In that life, I was about five-two or -three. I was bustier and a strawberry blonde, with almost porcelain skin. I looked like a pretty little china doll."

Popular in high school, Maureen was dating rather seriously when she graduated in 1972. "But I knew that a permanent relationship with any male other than my past-life husband would be out of the question," she said.

"What made you think he had even been incarnated during the same time sequence?" I asked.

She shrugged. "I just knew it. I had faith in my dreams."

"I guess you must have believed that faith has the power to move mountains or find past-life loves."

Maureen pursed her lips and sat for a moment or two in reflective silence. "I just always knew that one day I would find him again and that our great love would be rekindled."

I suggested that she had to have great inner resolve to be able to be sustained by a belief.

Maureen agreed. "I always believed with every fiber of my being that this man from the past would also be my destiny in my future. I knew he was out there somewhere."

A child of the sixties, Maureen admitted that she had longed to participate in significant peace marches in high school. However, teenaged hippies were something of a rarity in small Kansas towns—especially if they came from good middle-class families and had to be home by midnight. Her protests primarily consisted of wearing leather vests with Native American beadwork and worn jeans with the knees gone. Maureen developed a social conscience and went to college planning to enter either law or social work.

Dreams of her perfect past-life mate also went with her to college, but it wasn't until her first year of graduate school that she actually met him.

"Never will I forget that fateful day," Maureen said. "Never will I forget the culmination of all my dreams of yearning and desire."

It happened on a beautiful October afternoon in 1976. Maureen and the present embodiment of her past-life love nearly collided with one another in the stacks at the Northwestern University library.

"It was incredible," she said. "He looked exactly as he had appeared in my dreams. I suddenly somehow knew his present-life name as well. It was Todd.

"My heart was beating so fast that I really thought I would faint. I said his name, and I am sure that the sound came out like the croaking of a big bird."

Maureen recalled Todd's mouth had dropped open when she'd called him by name.

"He stood there gaping at the stranger who had just appeared before him and who'd dropped all the books she'd had in her arms." She giggled.

Todd frowned and asked how she knew his name.

"I've seen you . . . around campus," Maureen managed to tell him.

Todd studied her thoughtfully. "I don't know your name, but I think . . . I know you from *somewhere.*"

"I'm Maureen. Maureen Martinson."

He smiled. "All right, Maureen. Do we have a class together? You do look familiar to me."

She was encouraged by the tiny ripple of recognition in Todd's memory.

"But then I remembered that although he looked just the same as in my dreams, I looked *nothing at all* like I had in my past-life memories," Maureen said.

Todd continued to work on the mystery. "Did

we go to school together? I mean, way back in elementary school, or something? My family moved around quite a bit. Could it have been long ago, maybe?"

Maureen told him that it was long ago and far away.

"Let me buy you a cup of coffee," she said. "I mean, I nearly knocked you over. Come on. We can talk about it."

As they walked to a nearby coffee shop, Todd told Maureen that he was about to become engaged.

"My heart sank," she admitted. "I mean, I felt like it exploded, then sank. But I had come too far and waited far too long to let anything come between us, now that I had actually met him in the flesh. And I certainly wasn't going to let something like another woman take him away from me. At least, not without a damn good fight!"

Maureen said that she did not immediately come right out and tell Todd about their past-life relationship and her dreams about their union.

"I think I waited until he was at least on his third cup of coffee," she said. "Thank God, he didn't laugh at me. I really think that I would have punched him out if he had laughed."

Maureen knows that for a while Todd thought he'd met a "Dorothy" from Kansas who probably knew the Wizard of Oz and even had his unlisted telephone number in Emerald City.

"But he heard me out," she said. "He sat there and listened to me and heard all about the dreams about 'us' that had haunted me since childhood. Then he asked me to a movie that night.

"I really think that at the beginning of our relationship Todd thought I had managed to come up with the most original line he had ever heard to pick someone up, but it wasn't too long before memories of what seemed to be our past life together began to come into his own consciousness. Just before he kissed me for the first time, he looked deep into my eyes and said, 'Somehow, I know that I *do* know you.' "

Although Todd was working on his master's degree in education, he confessed that he had always liked to paint as a hobby.

"It wasn't until we had been seeing each other for several weeks that he showed me one of his paintings," Maureen said. "It still gives me goosebumps thinking about it. The first time I saw it, I nearly flipped out. It was of a stretch of beach and a small cottage. In front of the cottage stood a woman with strawberry blond hair and fair, white, almost porcelain skin. Todd could not explain why he had painted the scene, but he said that he had found himself in the strangest state of anticipation ever since he had completed the work. It was as if he had been waiting for destiny to tell him what was about to occur in his life. That was why he had heard me out that first night. On some deeper level of inner knowing, he had sensed that his life was about to change."

Maureen leaned back and glanced at her wristwatch. "Oh, goodness. I hope I haven't made you late for your next lecture."

I still had a few minutes. That evening I was

giving a demonstration in group regression. "So both you and Todd are convinced that you came together because of the past-life dreams of your childhood?"

Maureen smiled. "Yes, although after nine years of marriage and two beautiful daughters, I guess it really doesn't matter all that much how we came together."

A caseworker for the welfare department in a large Midwestern city, Maureen continued to exercise her concern for social issues. Todd taught American literature on the secondary level and painted in every spare moment. He most enjoyed doing portraits of his three lovely ladies.

As a postscript to our discussion, Maureen added, "Each morning I begin the day by asking my two girls, ages six and four, if they had any good dreams while they slept. I don't push it, but I'm curious to see if any of this can be transmitted genetically. I'm curious to see if either of them might begin to have dreams of her past lives—and her future husband."

Five

Being Together Out-of-the Body

Michele Kaplanak's husband, Ed, is a construction worker who once, due to the scarcity of local employment, was forced to take a job on a large dam project more than three hundred miles from their home.

"It was the longest six months I've ever spent," Michele said. "Ed could get home only on weekends. He would not arrive until after midnight on Friday, and he would have to be back on the road right after the noon meal on Sunday. For those six months, we lived only on Saturdays."

She remembered one dreary fall day when she was particularly lonely. The clouds hung low in the sky and drizzled on the leaves at sporadic intervals.

"It was the kind of day to share with someone you love," she said. "It was the kind of day to cuddle by an open fireplace."

She felt lonely and depressed, but she pulled on a heavy sweater and sat in her chilly house, pasting premium stamps in books.

"That night my bed felt as cold and damp and lonely as a grave," Michele said. "My only consolation was that it was Thursday night, and Ed would be home that next evening. I lay shivering between the sheets, cursing the job situation that had taken my husband so far away from me."

Then she thought she felt a slight pressure on Ed's side of the bed.

"I turned over and saw nothing, but it seemed to me that I could feel a kind of warmth coming from Ed's pillow."

She ran her hand along the inside of the sheets.

"For a crazy minute there, I feared that I might be losing my grip on reality," Michele said. "Ed's side of the bed most definitely felt warm, like he had been sleeping there and had just gotten up."

Michele lay on her side of the bed for a few moments longer, then, once again, she slid her hand over the sheet.

"There could be no mistaking it! The bed on Ed's side was as warm as toast," she reported.

It had been a lonely day for Michele. She had no interest in attempting to theorize *why* that side of the bed should be so warm when no one was sleeping there.

"Without another moment's hesitation, I slid over into the blessed pocket of warmth and comfort and fell fast asleep almost at once."

Michele really did not think of the strange incident again until three days later, when she and her husband were eating their farewell Sunday meal. Ed's response to her curious story was hardly what she had expected.

"He stared at me for a few moments in complete silence, as if uncertain how next to proceed. Then he spoke to me in slow, measured sentences and told me a most amazing story."

That Thursday night, Ed Kaplanak had been lying in the construction workers' bunkhouse, trying to come to terms with his loneliness.

"I really felt like chucking it all that night," he told Michele. "Job or no job, I just wanted to come home to you right then."

That night, as he lay there surrounded by his snoring bunkmates, Ed's entire being seemed suffused with personal anguish. He wanted so much to be in his own clean bed, to be able to feel Michele sleeping next to him.

"I decided to experiment," he told Michele. "I wanted to see if it were possible to will myself home over those three hundred miles. I rested my hands behind my head and summoned every ounce of concentration that I had inside my brain. I thought of nothing but you and home. I kept telling myself that it was possible to project my spirit to you. I have always believed that we were destined to be together and that all things would be possible for us—even this.

"There was a kind of rushing sensation, and I stood beside our bed, looking down at you. You were just lying there, looking kind of sad, not yet sleeping. I slipped into bed beside you, and you moved your hand over me. A few minutes later, you did it again. I thought that you knew I was there, because you rolled over and snuggled up next to me. I put my arm around you, and we both went right to sleep."

Michele stated in her report of the incident that

although Ed awakened back in the bunkhouse and she awakened alone in their bed back home, they will always wonder if Ed really did come home that night—or if their deep love enabled them to share a vivid dream so that they could experience a moment of comfort when they were both longing so terribly for one another.

A growing number of scientific researchers are becoming increasingly convinced that experiences similar to Michele and Ed Kaplanak's may truly be much more than exceptionally vivid dreams. The phenomenon of leaving one's body to manifest in spirit to float to the ceiling, to travel to another room—or in some cases, to another city or country—is known as astral travel or out-of-body experience.

Dr. Charles Tart, a psychologist and lecturer at the University of California at Berkeley, has noted that accounts of out-of-body experience (OBE) can be found throughout history.

"You can go into Egyptian tombs and see diagrams on the walls of how it is supposed to be done," Dr. Tart said. "Greek mystic religions apparently had techniques to induce this experience that were the crux of their initiation ceremonies. [OBE] seems to be an altered state of consciousness . . .

"In the Western world, we've rejected these states; we deny they exist, when in fact, we should be asking, 'Is ESP an evolutionary factor just coming in or just dying out?' In other cultures—

all Asia, almost—the altered states of consciousness are acknowledged and used."

Of the over 20,000 men and women who have
responded to the "Steiger Questionnaire of Mystical, Paranormal, and UFO Experiences," 74 percent reported having undergone out-of-body
experiences.

Psychic researcher Frederic W. H. Meyers saw
out-of-body experience as the manifestation of that
which is deepest and most unitary in the whole
being of the human entity. Dr. Meyers considered
OBE, of all vital phenomena, the most significant,
"the one definite act which . . . a person might
perform equally well before and after bodily
death."

The numerous accounts of spontaneous out-of-
body experience and the carefully conducted experiments in controlled mind projection seem to
demonstrate that the human psyche has the ability
to circumvent the physical limitations of time and
space. Although our physical bodies may have to
exist in a material world where the confining strictures of mass, energy, space, and time shape our
environment, it appears that an ethereal, spiritual
part of ourselves, our Essential Selves, are fully
capable of traveling free of our physical bodies.

Perla Margulies told me of the time when she
and her husband, Cody, had resided in an eastern
seacoast colony of painters, artists, poets, writers,
and visionaries.

"That was back in the early 1970s. We were
both in our mid-twenties and not yet married,"

she explained. "I had decided that I didn't want to be an elementary schoolteacher any longer. I wanted to be a painter. Cody had decided that he didn't want to be an accountant any longer. He wanted to be a singer.

"We met in Miami, Florida; and after a couple of months of seeing each other nearly every night, we had begun living together. We were completely convinced that we had been destined to meet in Miami . . . he from Wyoming, me from Oklahoma. Cody supported us by singing in different clubs and lounges, but we knew that it was our ultimate destiny to move on to bigger and better things. However, by the time we'd decided to move up north and try life in the artists' colony, I was pregnant."

Although they were both tuned into metaphysics and the paranormal, they approached the field of inquiry with very different ideals.

"I began to practice cosmic motherhood toward my unborn baby," Perla said. "I had really gotten into certain aspects of the Goddess movement, especially honoring the Earth Mother and walking a life path of love and balance. I also very much believed that my thoughts and my meditations would influence the character and the personality of the developing soul-entity within my womb. I shopped primarily at health food and natural produce stores; I meditated daily; and I tried to live a spiritual life as completely as possible."

Cody, on the other hand, found it difficult to follow a disciplined path. "Like so many other 'metafizzlers,' he wanted a quick fix," Perla explained. "He used to argue that he could find spirituality nice and easy by smoking dope. I warned him that he was following the path of illusion."

Perla became upset when she saw Cody beginning to experiment with certain occult practices that she had always considered to be negative and exploitive of other people.

"To make matters worse," she said, "Cody was unable to hide his fascination for a certain young woman, barely twenty, believed by some to be the High Priestess of a coven of self-styled witches."

Perla did not claim to be an expert on the old religion of Wicca, but it seemed apparent to her that the loosely organized coven that met under the young witch's direction had begun, perhaps ignorantly, toying with the dark side of the occult mysteries.

"So at this point," Perla said, "while I was seeking spiritual development and Cody sought kicks, we were still unmarried—and I was still very pregnant. Nearly every night Cody left to perform a gig at a local bar or lounge while I stayed home alone and watched my girlish figure become transformed into a blimp."

Cody usually stayed out well past the bar's closing time, so Perla was painfully aware that he was avoiding both her and his responsibility.

"What of our destiny together?" I would remind him. "We had such wonderful plans. Were we deceiving one another?"

Cody would then take her in his arms and beg for her understanding. "I just need some time. I'm going through a lot of heavy stuff right now. Of course you are my destiny, lovebug," he told her.

"Finally, when I was in my seventh month of pregnancy, Cody proposed marriage," Perla said. "I wept openly with joy and relief. I had resigned myself to being left alone to face motherhood."

However, it was soon sadly apparent that the mere vocalization of his commitment to the pregnant Perla had done little to domesticate the father-to-be.

"In spite of numerous tearful sessions, I could not convince Cody to stay at home during the day and to come directly home after his last set of the evening," Perla recalled. "I begged him to give me the crucial support and love I so desperately needed."

Perla began losing sleep, worried by her acute awareness that a woman in her advanced state of pregnancy would present little competition to the slim and lovely young things who frequented the bars and lounges where Cody sang.

"One evening, I was having a particularly difficult time coping with my ruptured reality," Perla said. "In an effort to divert my raw nerves and my damaged emotions, I began to sketch. My troubles with Cody had got me behind on a deadline for some artwork that I was doing for a local advertising agency, so I decided to try to catch up—since I knew sleep would be out of the question."

Perla found to her puzzlement that her pencils seemed to have a life of their own. A line here. Another there. A bit of shading.

"To my utter astonishment, the sheet of paper began to fill up with the face of an attractive young girl. I knew that I had never seen her before, but I also *knew* that the features before me comprised an exact rendering of a real person."

Perla slumped back in her chair as she began to receive impressions about the young woman whose portrait she had just sketched.

"She was barely eighteen. She had recently graduated from high school and was feeling very worldly out on the town with some friends. Cody, singing love songs in a cheap bar, had seemed the very epitome of sophistication in her innocent and limited worldview."

Then, as Perla stared at the portrait, something very, very strange occurred. "The paper became a swirling, fuzzy mass of images. I shook my head to clear it of its sudden weird feeling of lightness. I felt as though my entire consciousness was suddenly scrunched up somewhere near the top of my skull—*and then I was out of my body, floating up near the ceiling, looking down at my pregnant physical self.*

"I felt as though the real me, my spirit body, was being tugged and pulled. Colors and lights passed before my spiritual eyes. And then I was soaring through the night sky, moving, it seemed, toward the stars."

The next thing Perla saw was Cody.

"I was in the back seat of our car. Cody was driving with someone I could not see clearly. I could, however, see all too clearly that it was a woman."

Cody drove up to a motel and got out of the car. Perla strained to see who his companion was.

"The car door opened, and the girl whose picture I had just drawn stepped out.

"Although I loathed watching my lover's infidelity, something, some force, seemed to hold me near Cody and his pickup. Like an unseen voyeur, I entered the motel room and watched."

Perhaps, Perla has since worked it out in her mind, the force that held her in that motel room intended to remove all doubts about Cody's unfaithfulness and prompt her to act in a manner that would once and for all end her humiliation.

"With the last cries and sighs of their passion, my spirit self was drawn back to our apartment," Perla said. "When the colors and lights stopped swirling around me, I was once again sitting at my drawing board and staring at the portrait of the young woman whom Cody had been with."

Cody returned to their apartment at daybreak. Perla was still awake, still weeping, when the memory of seeing her lover in another's arms became too much to contain.

"I wasted no time in confronting him with his infidelity," Perla said. "When he denied any knowledge of what I was talking about, I flashed the portrait in his face. He blanched visibly and tried to regain his composure, but his eyes could not keep from straying toward the portrait."

About an hour later, the doorbell rang. Since Cody was angrily hunched over on his side of the bed, still vehemently denying everything, Perla got up to answer the door.

The sight of their caller almost made Perla recoil against the doorframe. There, wearing a simpering expression, was the girl.

"Is Cody home?"

Perla made an expansive sweep of her arm and

indicated a shocked, open-mouthed Cody hunched on the edge of the bed.

"I noted with grim satisfaction that the girl had become suddenly very subdued," Perla remembered. "She was intelligent enough to assess the role that I—very obviously pregnant and red-eyed from weeping—played in Cody's life. Without another word, she turned from the door of our apartment and ran away."

Cody got up and splashed some bourbon in a glass. "You knew, didn't you? You really knew. Somehow you saw it all tonight, didn't you?"

Perla lowered her eyes and began to weep again. "Some energy, perhaps my spirit guide, first took control of my hand and sketched her portrait. Then, somehow, I was taken out of my body and brought to the motel room where the two of you made love."

Cody's eyes brimmed with tears. "I've been a real creep! A total bastard! I've forgotten my vow to you. I've dishonored the destiny that we used to see so clearly.

"At this point, after the way I've behaved, the unforgivable things I've done, I realize that my words and my promises will mean nothing to you. Marry me right now, and I swear by all things bright and beautiful and holy that I'll be a changed man. I'll be a good husband and father."

Today Perla is a successful commercial artist and Cody has published a number of country songs that have enjoyed a modest popularity. They have two children.

"Perhaps the most amazing part of our story," Perla said, "is that I still agreed to marry Cody—

and that nearly twenty years later, we're still together. A little part of me will probably always wonder if Cody married me because he truly *did* come to believe in our destiny together—or if he figured he had better be good because my out-of-body eyes would always be upon him."

Closely linked to out-of-body journeys of the spirit are instances that may be *unconscious* projections of the etheric body. In these instances, men and women have been confronted by the apparitions of loved ones who still solidly reside within their fleshly shells. In other words, we are talking about "ghosts" of the living.

One evening, Brian Denomme had worked late. It was nearly midnight before he returned home. There were few lights left on in the house, but as he opened the door, he thought he caught a glimpse of Debbie, his wife of four months, hiding in a corner of the front room.

Believing that his playful wife wanted to tease him, Brian pretended not to see her, hoping to surprise her at her own game. He walked straight ahead for a few steps, then suddenly whirled around toward the spot where she crouched behind a piece of furniture.

Debbie managed to evade him, and she danced lightly out of reach of his arms.

Brian pursued her around the room, but she always moved just ahead of his grasp.

At last he darted forward and laughingly cornered her by the wall. He gave a shout of triumph, but as he was about to throw his arms around her, he heard a peculiar sound, like the report of a faraway rifle—and Debbie vanished before his astonished eyes.

He stepped back from the wall, his head literally throbbing as he tried to understand just what had happened.

"Brian, honey, is that you? Are you finally home?" It was Debbie's voice, coming from the bedroom.

But how could she be in the bedroom when she had just been running around, teasing him, in the living room?

"What was all that noise?" Debbie wanted to know. "What on earth are you doing out there?"

Brian found his wife in bed, where she insisted she had been all the time, having grown weary of waiting up for him.

The bizarre incident troubled Brian Denomme for three years until I explained ghostly doubles of the living to him after one of my lectures on psychic phenomena.

Jayne Langstaff saw her husband's astral double one night as he lay sleeping beside her.

"I was sleeping very restlessly that night," she remembered. "We had gone to bed too early, about ten o'clock; and now here it was only a little past midnight and I had awakened. As I turned my head toward Peter, I saw a most remarkable sight. His astral body, or soul, was rising out of his physical body. It was transparent, and it had a soft silver glow to it. While I watched, it sat up beside him for a moment, then it got up and walked toward the bathroom door."

Jayne knew that she was wide awake, but she didn't know for certain what was happening.

"I was kind of frightened," she admitted. "I mean, I didn't know if Peter had died and I was seeing his soul leaving me. I guess I was somewhat reassured when it headed toward the bathroom. I figured if Peter had died, his soul would head for someplace other than our bathroom."

At last she called out to the figure, asking Peter where he was going.

"It paid no attention to me. The physical Peter lay sleeping peacefully beside me. The astral body of my husband stood before the bathroom door, as if undecided whether or not to leave the bedroom.

"I was able to get a good look at Peter's astral body as it walked across the room. It was identical to his physical body—same reddish-colored hair, same pajamas, everything. Except, as I said, his astral body had a soft, silver glow around it, and it was transparent."

Jayne closed her eyes for a few moments and prayed that all was well with her husband.

"When I opened my eyes again, Peter's soul-body had returned to his physical body, and he lay sleeping restfully beside me."

In her account of the experience, Jayne Langstaff said that the incident convinced her that it is possible for the human soul to exist outside the body while the physical shell is asleep or in a deep trance. She also stated that the experience had provided her with personal proof that the human soul goes on living after the death of the physical body.

Six

Destined Love Sent from
Another Dimension

In June 1983, Greg Lovering was called back to the family home in Carmel, California, to be at the bedside of his dying mother.

"Dad had passed on five years before," Greg said. "I had just sold my interest in an East Coast advertising agency, so I was able to spend the last two weeks of Mother's life at her side.

"After the reading of the will and a number of family business matters were completed, I decided to take some personal time to 'find myself.' I didn't have to hurry back to work, because I had sold my business. The money I had made on that transaction, plus the inheritance from my mother, made it possible for me to embark on a journey of self-discovery.

"And there was no question that I was greatly in need of some time to reevaluate my life. I was thirty-five years old, and I could already chalk up two marriages, two divorces, and a recent broken engagement. Although I had made a lot of money,

I had lost even more. In the process of building and destroying two fortunes, I had managed to acquire ulcers, a spastic colon, and, from time to time, a very good imitation of a nervous breakdown."

Greg decided to drift around the area, rediscovering the scenic beauty of the Monterey Peninsula, visiting the lush vineyards, and frequenting the bustling fishermen's docks. He hoped to lose a morose spirit among the carefree people who visited these popular tourist attractions.

"I first saw Sofia Evangelista at one of those quaint outdoor cafés in Carmel," Greg said. "She was sitting alone, sipping pensively at her cup of tea. I was almost overcome with her elegance, her beauty, her poise. I could not believe that this dark-haired goddess could be alone. And although every man's eyes were on her, it seemed as though no one had the temerity to approach her."

No one, that is, except for Greg.

"When I asked if I might share her table, she looked up at me and smiled as if she had been sitting there just waiting for me to join her. Truly, it was as if we were already together and I had just returned to our table after using the telephone.

"Within minutes, I knew not only her name, but her age (twenty-nine), place of birth (La Jolla), and occupation (freelance photographer). We talked without pause over a splendid lobster dinner, continued our nonstop conversation over drinks, and were in the process of sharing our innermost secrets when our waiter begged our forgiveness and understanding, but the manager was insisting that the café really must close."

By that time Greg knew that he was in love as he had never been before.

"When we went back to my hotel room, I told Sofia that I felt our meeting had been destined, that everything that had ever happened to me—the good, the bad, the ghastly, the magnificent—had only been a prelude to the wonderful moment when I first saw her.

"Sofia agreed that we had been destined to meet. She said that it was as if she had been waiting for me to appear all her life."

Sofia became Greg's reason for living. She was in the area photographing scenic layouts for a national magazine. Day and night for two weeks they were with each other constantly.

"Never had I loved so intensely," Greg stated in his account. "Never before had I felt so completely that a woman loved me to the very fiber of my soul."

When Sofia sadly informed him that she had to return to New York soon with her photographs, Greg convinced her to send the pictures by Express Mail and to spend another week with him.

"I would have married her then," he said, "but she told me that she had been given the assignment for which she had yearned her entire career. A magazine with an international circulation was sending her to the Amazon rain forest to do a photo piece on the plight of the native people in the path of progress."

Since Greg had no work-related responsibilities at that time, he suggested that they get married, then travel to the Amazon on their honeymoon. He could be her willing pack-bearer and tote all her film rolls and extra lenses.

"Sofia told me that this assignment was something that she must do alone, on her own," he said. "She reminded me that I had told her that I was embarked on my own journey of self-discovery when I met her. This voyage to the Amazon, she said, would be a kind of vision quest for her."

Sofia warned Greg that she could be gone for as long as three months.

"I groaned that such a period of time seemed like an eternity to me, now that I had found her," Greg said. "I told her that I doubted I could stand being apart from her for so long.

"She became very serious, placed a forefinger on my lips to silence them, then told me that on the level of soul communion, we would always be together. 'My darling,' she said, 'we are two halves of a whole. We have been one since before time began. We shall be one forever.'"

Sofia promised to telephone whenever she could and to write as often as possible.

"She phoned me just as soon as her plane landed in Rio de Janiero. I received another call from somewhere in the interior about three days later. After a month, I got a hastily written letter from her. Then . . . nothing."

After Greg had heard nothing more from Sofia for six weeks, he called the magazine that had given her the assignment in the hopes that they might provide him with some additional information regarding Sofia's welfare.

"Some snide and pompous twit told me that

they could not give out information about any of
their reporters or photographers," Greg said, still
bristling at the insulting behavior. "Finally, some
officious-sounding person came on the phone and
said that she, to the best of her knowledge, had
never heard of a Sofia Evangelista."

Greg was both outraged and confused. A friend
in the publishing business reminded him how
often publication staffs experienced turnover of
personnel, so he might indeed have gotten connected with some editor who had never heard of
Sofia. On the other hand, she also advised Greg
that editorial staffs were very protective of their
writers and photographers. After all, he could have
been some nut trying to stalk Sofia while she was
on assignment.

Greg plunged into a period of dark and brood-
ing gloom.

"I leased an apartment in San Francisco, and I
began spending long hours with a number of
newly acquired friends. I simply did not wish to
be alone. I didn't know if my dear Sofia was alive
or dead. I kept torturing myself with the thought
that just as I'd met the love of my life while on
my journey of self-discovery, maybe Sofia'd met
the love of *her* life while on her vision quest in
the Amazon."

Five months passed. Two days before Christmas, Greg sat with two close friends discussing
philosophy, part of his mind, as always, on Sofia.
A knock sounded at his door, and when he answered it, he was astounded to see his beloved
Sofia.

"She seemed even more lovely than before—

serene, elegant, and amused by my obvious state of surprise and confusion. She was dressed almost completely in white, a color that accented her dark beauty. She wore gold high-heeled shoes, and a gold necklace, and as before, she allowed her magnificent black hair to fall to her shoulders."

The two lovers rushed to each other's arms, embracing wildly, dancing about the room in joyful spins and swirls. Greg's friends soon left them alone, after having been completely captivated by Sofia's charm and gentle personality.

"We talked endlessly," Greg said, "but each time I asked her how she'd been, why she hadn't communicated with me, or how she'd found my apartment, Sofia would say, 'Hush now, my darling. Be quiet. I'm here now, and that's all that's important.' "

When they went to bed that night, Greg held his dear Sofia tightly, as if fearful she might suddenly vanish.

Once, much later that night, he reached out for her and was reassured by her presence.

Sofia lay propped on an elbow, her dark, somber eyes gazing at him with love and kindness. When she asked him why he slept so restlessly, Greg answered her frankly: "Because I am afraid that you are going to vanish again. I am afraid that you will somehow vaporize . . . just disappear."

Sofia laughed at his fears and told him to go back to sleep.

"Yet that next morning, when I woke," Greg said, "my darling Sofia was gone!"

The bed where she had slept was still warm.
The pillow still held the shape of her head. But
Sofia was nowhere to be seen.

"It seemed impossible that she had been able
to get out of bed and leave the apartment without
awakening me," Greg said. "Especially since I
had been sleeping so fitfully with my fear of losing her once again."

Greg found a note on the nightstand. It was in
Sofia's handwriting and bore only the briefest of
messages—the name of a coffee shop, and these
words: *a surprise for you.*

Greg's heart lightened. Somehow, Sofia had
managed to leave his apartment, but she had indicated where she would meet him.

"When I entered the coffee shop, I immediately
spotted Sofia, sitting at a table in the back with
a handsome young man," Greg said. "I felt light-
headed and my knees almost buckled. If her surprise was to introduce me to the man with whom
she had fallen in love during her five months in
the Amazon, I knew I would never be able to bear
it."

Greg tried his best to calm himself, but he heard
his voice quavering when he stood at the table.
"Sofia, I . . . I am here for my surprise. I hope
it will be one I will like."

She looked up at him with no sign of recognition. "I beg your pardon, sir?"

The young man was immediately wary, defen-
sive, and protective. "Do you know this man,
Sis?"

Sis? Thank God, the handsome young man was
Sofia's brother!

"Sofia," Greg wanted to know, "why are you looking at me so strangely?"

The beautiful woman smiled as the scene began to make sense to her. "Oh, you have mistaken me for my cousin Sofia. Our mothers were sisters. People say that Sofia and I look enough alike to be twins. I am Gloria Perez."

This was moving a bit too fast for Greg, and he asked permission to sit down.

"I'm sorry," Gloria said. "You appear shocked. Did you know Sofia well?"

Why was the question asked in the past tense? "What do you mean, *did* I know her?"

"He doesn't know," she said to her brother. Then, redirecting her attention to Greg, she told him in a soft, gentle voice, "Our dear Sofia died last June after a long illness."

Greg asked for a glass of water, and then, cautiously at first, began to tell Gloria and her brother Ray the entire story.

Although they were obviously shocked at his claim that he had spent the night before with Sofia, he showed them the note that had directed him to them that morning, and they silently agreed to hear him out.

"Is it possible for other people to share someone's hallucination?" Greg challenged them. "My two friends saw Sofia last night. They'll tell you that I'm not making all of this up. Sofia has been with me many times. To me she was warm, real, full of love and life."

Greg arranged for Gloria and Ray to hear the testimonies of his two friends, who were astonished to learn that they had met a ghost. "We each saw her with our own two eyes," they swore.

As they entered Greg's apartment building, he played a hunch that his maintenance man might have seen Sofia.

"Gil," he asked him, "did you happen to notice any of my guests last night?"

The man laughed at what seemed a nonsensical question. "D'ya mean the two gents, or this pretty young lady standing beside you? That was some terrific white dress you had on, miss, if you don't mind my saying so."

Gloria blanched at the man's comment. "Do you mean to say that you saw *me* here last night?"

Gil became flustered, then angry at Greg. "Don't get me involved in nothin', man. So who's this other guy? Her angry husband, I suppose."

"Relax, man," Ray told him. "I'm her brother. And I'm not angry. I'm just thinking what a wonderful Christmas present Sofia has given all of us."

Gloria's eyes misted over and she nodded her agreement. "You're right, Ray. She's just shown all of us that life goes on. That we do survive the grave."

Greg concluded his remarkable account on the positive note that Sofia's Christmas present extended beyond the season.

"I spent Christmas Eve with the Perez family, and after a couple of dinner dates, Gloria and I began seeing each other seriously. We took things very cautiously, and we were married in August of 1985.

"I would never be so callow as to compare individuals, but Gloria seemed to embody all the wonderful attributes with which Sofia had so charmed me. Plus, she has the added attraction that she never disappears."

Who—or *what*—was Sofia Evangelista?

Was she a restless spirit who had been cut short in her own Earth life and who sought to live vicariously through her cousin?

Was she an angelic being who assumed the physical appearance of the deceased Sofia in order to bring Greg together with his true destiny, Gloria?

Could she have been the soul-entity of one of Greg's past-life loves, manifesting in spirit form to bring him together with Gloria, another past-life lover to whom he owed a karmic debt?

Or, as one metaphysician theorized, could Sofia have been a personified projection of Greg's own psyche—literally, his "other half," his feminine self—that manifested for the sole purpose of guiding him to Gloria, his destined love?

Of the over 20,000 respondents to our "Steiger Questionnaire of Mystical, Paranormal, and UFO Experiences," 48 percent are convinced that they have seen a ghost; 42 percent state that they have perceived the spirit of a departed loved one; and 60 percent claim to have witnessed a variety of spirit entities.

While the case of Greg and the materialization of the entity Sofia directing him toward his true destined love, Gloria, is one of the most intriguing accounts in my files, the experience of Carol Larson Hickok is quite similar and equally eerie in its multilevel implications.

* * *

When Carol was a junior in high school, her parents moved out into the country, forcing her to leave her friends back in the city.

"In those days (the early 1950s), schoolbuses didn't travel far beyond the municipal limits of the medium-sized South Dakota city from which we had moved, and I found myself attending a much smaller township school. Every couple of weeks, my mother would take my sister Laura and me back to the city to borrow books from the library. I felt completely removed from my old school friends, except for an occasional chance meeting among the quiet library stacks. And because Mom would usually be back to pick us up after a hurried visit to the supermarket, there was never much time to maintain friendships."

One day at the library, about a year after her family had moved to the country, Carol quickly selected the books that she wished to check out, then sat on the library steps to await her mother's return.

"I had not sat there long," she recalled, "when I saw the familiar figure of Ronnie Broderson, a boy from my class in the city high school approaching. He was a handsome boy, a good athlete, and I remembered how all the girls always made a fuss over him. Just seeing him reminded me how miserable I was in that little township high school. There weren't any boys like Ronnie there."

Carol could hardly contain her excitement when she saw Ron really was walking in her direction.

"Hey, Carol," he called out, when he spotted her sitting on the library steps. "It is you, isn't it? Carol Larson? Boy, you've gotten even prettier since you moved. Must be that country living."

Carol remembered blushing and feeling embarrassed. "But I was putty in Ronnie's hands. I offered little resistance when he asked me to walk across the street to the park and sit on a bench with him. I had had a crush on Ronnie since fourth grade. We dated once when we were sophomores, just a plain, old unromantic movie date. I had always hoped for more, but I pretty much decided that Ronnie didn't really like me all that much.

"When we settled ourselves on the bench, Ronnie put his arm around my shoulders and my heart started thudding so hard it hurt. I thought I would faint when he bent down and kissed me on the cheek!"

Ronnie told her that he had always liked her. "I was sure sorry when you and your folks moved."

Carol said that she'd missed all the kids at first, but some of her new friends were nice, too. "I just wish there were some handsome boys like you out there. Boys I could care for the way I . . . I cared about you."

She felt instantly awkward and embarrassed once she had just come right out with her feelings about him.

"That's real nice of you to say that, Carol," Ron said. "As I said, I always liked you. But there's one boy out there in your school who I think is really neat. I know I like him, and I think you would, too."

"Who's that?" Carol asked, not really wanting to know. She had begun to create the most beautiful mental images of Ronnie and her writing love letters back and forth and meeting when she came into the city. She had even fashioned a perfectly marvelous picture of Ronnie driving down their lane in his old Ford.

"Bob Hickok," Ron answered her indifferent query.

Carol laughed. "Wild Bob?" She used the nickname the kids had taken from the Old West gunfighter, Wild Bill Hickok.

"Now, now," Ron scolded. "Bob gets teased enough about that. He's really a terrific guy."

Carol finally admitted that Bob was "kind of cute," but she kept wondering how she could maneuver the conversation back to *them* and getting Ronnie to come driving down their country lane.

"Are you going with anyone, Ronnie?" she asked, knowing that every minute counted, since her mother would soon be coming.

Ronnie surprised her by laughing heartily in response to her bold question. "Not any more. There's no need. You see, I'm going to go away from this town, too."

Carol's heart sank. "You . . . you're moving away?"

Ron sighed and tightened his one-armed embrace of her shoulders. "Far away, kid. Far, far away. You're never going to see this old boy ever again."

Carol remembered feeling terribly depressed, and she thought for certain that she would begin to cry. The image of Ronnie's Ford coming down their lane evaporated into a murky mist.

"How about a goodbye kiss?" Ron asked gently. "A farewell kiss for an old friend who's going to go far, far away."

This time, Ron kissed Carol on the lips. "He held the kiss for so long that I thought I really would faint this time."

When he finally released her, Carol looked up into the scowling features of her mother and the laughing face of Laura.

"Mama grabbed me by the hand, and I barely had time to wave goodbye to Ronnie before she dragged me off to the car," Carol said. "Ronnie was grinning from ear to ear. 'Don't forget to be nice to my friend Bob,' he yelled after us. 'Bob is a great guy. You two are made for each other!'"

Carol said she'd never forget the argument that she and her mother had all the way home that night.

"Finally, when I explained that Ronnie was going to be moving away and Laura supported my claims that he was a great guy, Mama became somewhat more understanding and sympathetic. She made it very clear, however, that she did not approve of any daughter of hers smooching on a bench in a public park."

It was nearly three weeks before Carol got back to the city and the library. Illness and farmwork had prevented her mother from taking them to

town any sooner. Carol had begun looking at Bob
Hickok with totally different eyes. He was a tall,
ruggedly handsome boy, and since they were both
juniors, they were together in most of their
classes. It was becoming obvious that Bob was
taking quite an interest in her as well.

By the time they got back to the library, they
knew the books would have overdue fines. Celeste
Motters, one of Carol's former classmates, was
working at the library desk, and as Carol was paying the late charges, she could not resist boasting
to Celeste about her rendezvous with Ronnie
Broderson in the park.

"That's in really bad taste, kid," Celeste said.
"Did you lose all your class, moving out with the
chickens and the pigs?"

Carol's temper flared. "Just a bit jealous, are
we, Celeste? Then you'll just be delighted to know
that Ronnie kissed me while we sat on a park
bench."

"Wow!" Celeste exclaimed, momentarily forget-
ting all about the QUIET sign over her head.
"Either you're getting goofy out on that farm—or
you are just getting plain crude!"

The head librarian came to shush the girls, and
Carol's former classmate turned to walk away
from her.

"Don't go, Celeste!" Carol whispered sharply,
catching her friend's arm. "We always got along
so well! Why do you accuse me of bad taste and
call me goofy or crude because I let Ronnie kiss
me? Is it just jealousy, or what?"

Celeste fixed her with a cold stare; then something within Carol's eyes caused her to thaw just

a bit. "Look, Carol, we all tell fibs now and then. No big deal. But it was in bad taste to talk about Ronnie Broderson kissing you a couple of weeks ago. Maybe you didn't know because you live out in the country now, but Ronnie was killed in an automobile accident almost five months ago."

Carol could find no words to utter as she watched the back of her friend moving away from her. *Ronnie, dead?* It simply could not be.

She recognized another former classmate across the library reading room and nearly ran to the table where the girl sat flipping through a magazine. She sadly confirmed the news of Ron's death.

"I can provide no logical, rational explanation of my experience that will please everyone," Carol said, concluding her report. "I only know that forty years ago, I had an encounter with an affectionate ghost. I know that I sat on that park bench and received a warm kiss from a boy who had been dead for nearly five months—and I can offer the additional testimony of my mother and my sister, who saw Ron Broderson as clearly as I felt him.

"We could never really understand why Ronnie's ghost played Cupid for me and Bob Hickok. He and Bob weren't related, and Bob said he couldn't remember ever meeting Ron.

"Bob and I went together through our junior and senior years in high school, and we got married three years after graduation. We have two wonderful kids.

"Maybe it wasn't really Ronnie's ghost, but an angel that came to me disguised as the handsome boy I'd had a crush on. Maybe the angels decided it was our destiny to be together, and they used Ronnie to work it all out."

Seven

Fated to Be His True Love's
Guardian Angel

One of my favorite stories from my files of those destined to love one another is about a man who became his lover's guardian spirit when an untimely fatal accident separated them.

Doreen Raney told me that she and Kevin Lawsky had known each other for many years and had become good friends long before they had begun to think romantically about each other.

"We had worked together in the same insurance company for nearly three years before we had a sudden awareness of each other as sweethearts," Doreen said. "There had been many times in the past when I had even taken my love-life problems to trusty and dependable Kevin, who at that time had seemed like a brother, someone in whom I could confide. Suddenly one evening after work, when we were sitting in his car just talking, he leaned over and kissed me—and that was that!"

Once they'd begun dating, Doreen soon learned

that Kevin had a mystical side to his nature. "He would philosophize about why some Force-Greater-than-We had for some reason chosen to keep us apart, yet together, for so long. He wondered why, though we were attracted to one another as close friends, we had seemed more like brother and sister than lovers."

One night as they relaxed with wine and cheese in front of the fireplace in his apartment, Kevin theorized that maybe he had been Doreen's brother in another lifetime. Doreen had laughed, not completely certain if Kevin was serious. "You mean, like in reincarnation? Other lifetimes? That sort of thing?"

"Sure." Kevin grinned, refilling her glass. "Why not? All things are possible."

"All things are possible," she agreed.

Kevin suggested that they close their eyes, relax, and allow their minds to drift. "Maybe we can pick up on a time when we really *were* brother and sister."

Doreen took another sip of her wine and lay her head back on Kevin's chest. She felt as if she were a kid playing "let's pretend."

"I'm kind of picking up a really romantic period," Kevin said, "like Renaissance Italy. I think I was a painter, and I created a portrait of you in an elegant, flowing gown. It caused a sensation because you were so beautiful and I was so talented. Your portrait made me famous overnight."

Doreen laughed at the dual conceit of her beauty and his talent. "And I was your *sister?*"

Kevin squeezed his eyelids tighter together. "Wait. It's coming clearer. Aha! Got it! You were my best friend's sister. At first, I felt very protective toward you, like a brother. Then, later, as I became increasingly rich and famous, we fell deeply in love."

Doreen sat up, laughed at him over the rim of her wineglass. "You're a little strange, you know that, don't you?"

Kevin shrugged. "The really weird part is that we had thirteen children. Six boys and seven girls."

Doreen picked up a sofa pillow to pummel him. "You should have kept your brotherly feelings toward me. Thirteen kids! You satyr!"

Kevin sighed. "Well, it could have been. Who can say?" Becoming serious, he said, "I only know that in this lifetime, the moment I first saw you, I felt very protective toward you. It was as if I wanted immediately to appoint myself your bodyguard."

Doreen snuggled up next to him. "Well, mister, you can guard my body forever."

"I will," he assured her, murmuring into her ear. "I will always protect you and look after you."

"When Kevin proposed to me, I did not hesitate to say yes," Doreen said. "He was twenty-eight; I was twenty-five. We were both old enough to know what we were doing—and young enough to enjoy doing it. We had not *fallen* in love; we had *grown* in love. Ours was the kind of ideal relationship that I had always read about in the women's magazines. Kevin and I had been friends before we'd become lovers."

Two months before their wedding date, Kevin was killed instantly in an automobile accident.

Doreen said that she had little memory of the first few weeks after Kevin's death.

"I was left to try to put back together the pieces of what seemed to be an irrevocably shattered life.

"It was well over a year before I began dating again, and I know that I was really hard on the men who asked me out. In my mind, no one could ever begin to compare to Kevin. No one could ever satisfy me on as many levels as Kevin had. There were a few men with whom I didn't mind being friends, but I was not ready to consider any of them as potential lovers."

Two years after Kevin's fatal accident, Doreen began to date Charles Mybeck.

"After three months, he asked me to marry him. I was unable to give him an answer, and asked for a few days to consider his proposal. I had tender feelings for Charlie, but I still felt I was not yet ready to marry." Doreen explained her feelings to him, but he continued to court her.

"Finally, after we'd been going together for nearly a year, I agreed to marry Charlie. He was a good-looking guy, probably better looking than Kevin had been. But in spite of his impeccable manners, Charlie did not have the depth of feeling that Kevin had shown me."

One night, less than a week before the wedding, Doreen lay tossing and turning in bed, unable to sleep.

"My mind was full of thoughts of Kevin. I fig-

ured it was kind of strange for a bride-to-be to
be thinking about her dead fiancé, rather than her
living husband-to-be; but I just lay there thinking
about what might have been.

"I started wishing that Kevin was right there
with me to talk the whole business over. Should
I marry Charlie, or shouldn't I? I knew he'd be
able to give me good advice, just as he had so
many times in the past."

She began to cry, and in between her sobbings,
she gradually became aware of Kevin's voice calling her name.

"I sat bolt upright in bed, struck with the sudden realization that I was not just imagining the
sound of Kevin's voice, I was really hearing him
calling to me! I looked in the direction from
which his voice seemed to be coming, and I was
startled to see him standing just as solid as life
next to the dresser."

So many images began to flood Doreen's brain
that she feared she might succumb to the shock
of seeing Kevin standing there and faint dead
away.

"I became strangely calm at the sound of his
voice. He told me my marriage to Charlie Mybeck
would be a serious mistake, that I must not marry
the man. 'He's not the man for you,' Kevin said.
'He's not what he appears to be.' "

Doreen said that she was so moved, so impressed by the apparition of her dead fiancé, that
she feigned illness and told Charles that they must
postpone their marriage until she had recuperated.

"Two weeks to the day that Kevin had appeared
to warn me that Charles Mybeck was not who he

pretended to be, he was arrested." Doreen and many others who had only seen one side of Mybeck were shocked by the charges of unsavory activities and his disturbing marital history.

"Two years later, just a few days before I turned thirty, Joel Raney asked me to marry him," Doreen said. "Joel was a kind, thoughtful man who from the very first had reminded me of Kevin. I felt almost certain that an apparition of my dear friend and lover would once again appear to let me know if my choice in men was a wise one.

"Three nights before my August wedding to Joel, Kevin appeared in my room. Once again, he looked just as solid as he had in life and as he had when he'd materialized to warn me about Charlie.

"I was not shocked this time, and I waited eagerly for some sign, some signal from him. This time, he only smiled at me, waved a hand, and disappeared.

"I knew," Doreen said, concluding her story of a love that had survived the grave, "that my dear Kevin had given my marriage to Joel his blessing and that he had waved his hand in a final farewell."

Eight

The Spirit Gives Permission

Just before Jennifer Jonsson moved in with Marshall Satern, she was warned by some of his friends that she should never bother to have marriage plans in her future. At least, not to Marshall.

"That's fine if you want to move in together," Karyn Petrovsky told her one day over lunch. "Just don't have your heart set on marrying the guy."

Jennifer nibbled on some celery and cream cheese. "Why? You know he's the marrying kind. He was married before."

Karyn nodded. "That's just it. He was devoted to Susan during her long illness, and especially after she suffered the stroke."

"She was so young." Jennifer frowned. "Thirty-three, thirty-four, something like that."

"Only thirty-two. Susan had always been jealous of Marshall. After her stroke, when she lost the ability to speak, she got worse, and very possessive," Karyn said.

Karyn probed her salad with her fork. Jennifer

could sense that she was trying to decide whether or not she should share something. After a few moments of silence, Karyn sighed and revealed some information that probably should have remained unknown to Jennifer.

"Once when Ken and I were visiting Marshall and Susan just a few days before she had the stroke, she started talking about life after death. Everyone knew she had been ill for some time and that her doctors had not been optimistic in their prognosis. We had heard that she'd developed complications and had only a few months to live. We tried to change the subject. It was morbid for someone so ill to be discussing funerals and such, but she continued talking on and on about what the afterlife must be like.

"Then she turned to Marshall and told him that she would come back to haunt him if he should ever remarry."

Jennifer felt a chill run through her. "Oh, I'm certain she must have been making some sort of joke."

"A joke in very bad taste," Karyn said somberly. "We tried to laugh it off at the time. But if you had seen the look in her eyes . . ."

Karyn could not suppress an involuntary shudder. She reached for her wineglass, and Jennifer saw that her hand was trembling.

"But surely Marshall would not take such a threat seriously," Jennifer protested.

Karyn had drained her glass and reached for the carafe to pour herself a refill. "After Susan's stroke . . . and her subsequent death, I think he learned to take it seriously. There are . . . things that go on in that house. I've heard them myself."

Jennifer felt a slight flush of anger. "Now you're trying to scare me. You're beginning to sound like a Gothic romance. You know, the scene where the new mistress of the mansion is warned about the master's terrible secret."

Karyn picked up the check and began to rise. Before she left the table, however, she took Jennifer's hand. "I'm sorry, dear. Truly I am. I've talked on and said far too much. The wine, I suppose. You know that Susan and I were dear friends. I sincerely wish you well, Jennifer. I like you. And Marshall certainly deserves some happiness in his life."

"I thought Karyn Petrovsky's comments to be in bad taste, and I hoped it was not her intention to undermine my relationship with Marshall," Jennifer said. "At first I didn't take her warning about Susan's malediction seriously, but during my first night in Marshall's home, I began to reconsider her words."

Jennifer and Marshall were preparing for bed one night when they heard a loud thumping sound from the room that Susan had occupied during the last months of her illness. Because of her stroke and her inability to speak, she had been forced to knock on the wall whenever she needed something.

"Marshall muttered something about a loose shutter," Jennifer said, "but I could see that he was very pale and shaken."

He breathed a deep sigh, as if he regretted the tradition that required the menfolk to investigate all strange night noises. He fastened the belt of his bathrobe securely about his waist, then stepped out into the hall.

"I sat nervously on the edge of the bed," Jennifer recalled. "I had resolved to give up smoking, but I snagged a butt from Marshall's pack on the nightstand. After a few minutes, the terrible pounding sound stopped.

"I turned to glance at the door and was startled to see a colorless, bony hand reach around the door and shut out the lights.

"I lost it," Jennifer admitted. "I sat there screaming until Marshall came back into the bedroom and snapped on the lights."

There were no further manifestations that night, but Jennifer told Marshall the next morning at breakfast that she did not want to sleep another night in that bedroom.

"Marshall agreed without a word of argument," she said. "He told me that as soon as he returned from work the next evening he would help me move the furniture to a back bedroom."

A freelance artist, Jennifer had set up her easel and sketch board in the front room, where there was a lot of natural light. Now, she was beginning to regret that she would not be leaving the house to go to work.

Marshall had only been gone a few minutes, when a flurry of knockings and thumpings sounded throughout the house.

"The venetian blinds actually shook as if they were caught in a heavy breeze," Jennifer reported. "I was certain I could hear the sounds of things being moved around in the attic.

"I didn't think I'd be able to go on living in that house. It seemed obvious to me there was something living in the shadows that did not want me there.

"Karyn had not just been making silly girltalk about Susan promising to come back to haunt Marshall. Somehow, Susan's spirit was still in the house, and it was apparent that she didn't mind haunting me as well."

Jennifer decided to stick it out.

"For several days the pattern of the haunting didn't vary," she said. "There would be thumpings at bedtime, and knockings and scrapings during the day.

"On a number of occasions, as I worked in the kitchen, I heard what sounded like a sick person dragging her feet up the stairs. Whenever I pushed open the kitchen door and looked up the stairs, however, there was never anyone there."

Jennifer had tolerated the eerie manifestations for more than a week when she heard a loud pounding emanating from Susan's bedroom.

"I got up from my sketch board and glanced up the stairway. I saw nothing, but there had been a rather dramatic departure from what I had come to accept as part of the haunting's regular schedule. Up until that afternoon, the pounding from Susan's bedroom had sounded only at bedtime."

Jennifer continued to watch the top of the stairs. If she had not known for certain that she was alone in the house, she'd have sworn that there truly was an invalid in that bedroom who was trying desperately to signal her.

"The longer I concentrated on the sounds coming from Susan's bedroom, the more I became convinced that her spirit was actually attempting to communicate with me."

Although she has since stated that she will never know how she managed to summon the courage, Jennifer walked up the stairs and entered the bedroom where Susan had lived her last days.

"I don't know what I expected to see. I guess I feared I'd be confronted with the ghostly image of the poor, sick woman whose place and home I had taken."

Jennifer remembered that the room still had an antiseptic smell to it.

"It was apparent that the room had received only a superficial cleaning after Susan's death. I stood there in the middle of it, not really having the faintest idea what my next move should be."

A loud thump sounded next to the bed.

"Startled, I turned quickly, nearly losing my balance. Another thud sounded from the wall next to the bed where the poor dying woman must have lain and rapped out her pitiful signals to her part-time nurses."

To her complete astonishment, an envelope appeared to flutter down from somewhere. "It looked like an autumn leaf dropping from a tree. It simply fluttered down from some invisible hiding place."

Jennifer picked it up and saw that it was a letter Susan had written to Marshall. "It was sealed and had never been read by Marshall."

That night she gave the letter to him. Hesitantly, he took the envelope from her hands. "Tears streamed unashamedly down his cheeks as he read the letter," Jennifer said.

"When he had regained his composure, he told me that Susan must have written the letter just hours before her death. She told him how much she loved him and she prayed that he would forgive her for some of the selfish and thoughtless things she had written in bitterness during the course of her illness.

"When she had been deprived of her voice after the stroke, she had been forced to do more listening and more thinking. Contrary to what Marshall had feared and Karyn had supposed, Susan wrote that she hoped that he *would* remarry. But she begged him always to remember her with kindness and to think only of the good days they had shared."

According to Jennifer Jonsson Satern, she and Marshall still live in the same house, but they never again heard the eerie knockings and thump ings from Susan's room. They have been married for seven years.

"I don't really think that the surviving personality of my husband's first wife was ever trying to drive me away," Jennifer concluded, "but I do think that she wanted to make her position clear to me and to Marshall. It was as though she would not permit, or sanction, Marshall's remarrying until he had read her last letter to him."

Nine

Earthbound Spirit Releases
Him to New Love

One of the most dramatic stories I have ever heard regarding two destined lovers and their encounter with the spirit world was told to me many years ago by an elderly spirit medium whom I have agreed to call "Sarah Woodward" to protect her privacy.

In 1921, Sarah married a rancher who lived in the Southwest. Chad Woodward had been a widower for nearly five years. He was a tall, ruggedly handsome man who owned a comfortable spread of grazing land and several hundred head of cattle. Matronly cupids in the county had been trying to play matchmaker for Chad for so long that they had almost given up on him and stamped "not interested" across his forehead.

However, when he returned from a trip to Saint Louis with Sarah, his lovely new bride, his friends' wives once again felt that all was right with the world and held a happy chivaree for the newlyweds.

"After the chivaree, all the neighbors gave us their blessing and left us alone to enjoy our first night together in Chad's large ranch house." Sarah smiled at the memory. "I could not help overhearing the women clucking over what a quiet, soft-spoken, sensible lady I appeared to be. Well, I like to think that I was all those things, but I didn't feel that I could tell Chad or any of those nice ladies and courtly gentlemen that I was also something a good deal more than what I seemed."

Sarah possessed a secret she had not even shared with her husband. For several years before her marriage, she had been a well-known spirit medium in Cincinnati. Just a few months before she had met Chad, she had decided to disavow her mediumship and move to Saint Louis to begin a new life.

"I had found the physical and mental drain of mediumship to be too great for my rather frail constitution, and I had grown sad and weary of watching the eligible men pass me by in favor of more orthodox wife material. I was working as a very conventional shopgirl in a clothing store when Chad met me."

That night, more than ever, as her husband took her in his arms, Sarah was glad she had decided to keep her mediumship a secret. Even though Chad's rugged features made him appear that he would not be frightened by any earthly man or beast, she would not have wanted to do anything unearthly to scare him away.

"I was soon to learn, however, that my husband also harbored a secret he had kept from everyone," Sarah said. "We were preparing for bed when I was startled to see a woman walk unannounced into our master bedroom."

As Sarah watched in astonishment, the woman strode to the middle of the room, narrowed her eyes, and glared at her, obviously seething with rage.

Sarah looked at her husband, expecting him to speak to the woman, whoever she was—neighbor, relative, friend, or jilted sweetheart.

"But Chad seemed to be unaware of her presence," Sarah recalled. "Admittedly, I was unfamiliar with the local customs, but it seemed to me that invasion of privacy was rude no matter where one lived."

It was clear to Sarah that the woman had no business storming into their bedroom, so she decided to tell her so. "What do you want in this room?" she demanded. "All the guests have gone home."

Chad chuckled and turned to her somewhat awkwardly. "They sure have, sweetheart. I guess they figure that we're still kind of on our honeymoon. It was thoughtful of everyone to leave so early and leave us all alone."

He seemed oblivious to the intruder's presence.

"Dear." Sarah frowned her impatience. "We are not alone."

The woman had put her hands on her hips and had begun to tap an angry foot on the hardwood floors.

Chad turned in surprise from the clothes closet, where he had been hanging up his suit. "What are you talking about, hon? There's no one here but us. Everyone has left."

Sarah realized her husband could not see the woman. *She was in spirit.* Sarah had time only to shout a warning before the angry uninvited visitor from the spirit plane hurled a vase at Chad's head. He fielded the heavy glass vase on his left shoulder and it crashed to the floor, shattering into a dozen pieces.

"Louise! Louise!" Chad shouted in the direction from which the vase had been thrown. "Please stop!"

Sarah sensed that the violent psychic storm had abated, and as "Louise" left the bedroom, she passed a cold chill over Chad that made him shiver. The rancher sat on the edge of the bed and began to weep.

"She has a nasty temper, doesn't she?" Sarah said, after several moments of silence.

Chad's eyes pleaded for Sarah's understanding. "She . . . warned me that something like this would happen if . . . if I ever remarried. I've known she was still in the house . . . I've felt her presence on and off these five years since she died."

Sarah nodded. Chad didn't really need to tell her these things. She had already received strong psychic impressions that told her much of what he was saying. But she knew it would do him good to talk about it.

"Well," she said with a sigh, "Louise is certainly one redhead who really lives up to the reputation for having a quick temper." As soon as she had spoken the words, Sarah regretted having opened her mouth.

"How did you know Louise had red hair?"

Chad was looking at her quizzically. "Surely none
of the women here tonight would have been so
rude as to tell you about Louise. Or did they?"

"No," Sarah assured him. "All of your friends
were on their best behavior. No one said a word
about your late wife."

Chad reached in his back pocket for a handkerchief. "You acted from the very first as if you
could see her. You were talking to someone in the
room before the disturbance began. Sarah," he demanded, "could you see her?"

Sarah admitted that she had seen Louise in
spirit form.

Chad wiped away his tears with the white handkerchief, then blew his nose. "But how? How
could you *see* her?"

Sarah chose to ignore the question. She knelt
and began to pick splinters of glass from the floor.
"Darling," she began in a soft voice. "I've always
been able to see men and women like Louise.
Ever since I was a little girl."

"You can see *ghosts?*" Her husband's voice
sounded as if it had come from within a deep
cavern.

"Sometimes I can see men and women who are
in spirit. A spirit such as Louise has remained
earthbound . . . probably because she felt possessive toward you while she was in the physical
body. She was strong and proud, and she was
taken away from you and from her life when she
was young."

Chad nodded, silently agreeing.

"What people call 'ghosts,' are usually the restless spirits of those who died violent deaths and

who cannot adjust to their sudden change of condition. In other cases, they are the spirits of men and women who are tied to the earth plane because of deeds left undone, lessons left unlearned—or because of earthly attractions that remain too strong."

Her husband leaned forward, cradled his head in trembling hands. She had not intended to say so much.

"Sarah," Chad spoke at last. "Can . . . can you also *talk* to ghosts?"

She considered her answer very carefully before she answered his question. "I am . . . I used to be . . . I used to be a spirit medium."

Chad could not suppress a sudden scowl. "You mean, you had a tent at carnivals and fairs and such, and told fortunes for people?"

"Of course not! I gave readings for a select clientele in my home or gave spirit messages in spiritualist churches in Ohio. Anyway, I gave all that up before I moved to Saint Louis."

"But you could *see* Louise," he reminded her.

Sarah had already considered this. Somehow, she had known that the gift of mediumship could not be surrendered so easily. Somehow she had known that her renunciation of a talent nurtured within her psyche by spiritual forces could not be accomplished as simply as resigning from a regular job. She knew now that she would remain a spirit medium until whoever had bequeathed her with such gifts decided to withdraw them.

Chad took her hands in his own and clasped them with his strong fingers. She knew what he

was going to ask before he had found the courage
to voice the words.

"Sarah, dear, could you . . . talk to Louise and
ask her to please leave us alone? I mean, I did
love her once, but now . . ."

He could no longer speak, but Sarah understood. He was a lonely man who sought to make
a new life for himself with a new bride.

"I walked the hallways of the ranchhouse that
night," Sarah said. "But I could neither see nor
sense any sign of Louise. I searched every room
and closet in the sprawling house, but it soon became apparent that the angry spirit of Louise had
spent its wrath for that night.

"I told Chad I was quite certain Louise would
return the next night when we prepared to go to
bed. As an earthbound spirit, Louise would feel
most jealous about her husband's intimate relationships, the ones she would least wish him to share
with another woman."

Neither Sarah nor Chad felt like attempting to
make love that night. Louise had won the first
round.

Sarah's prediction proved true. The next night,
as she and Chad were undressing for bed, she
caught sight of Louise's spirit manifesting in the
bedroom.

"Louise was shaking an angry finger at Chad,
and I knew that the psychic fireworks were about
to begin," Sarah said. "I shouted at the spirit being to listen to me."

The spirit turned to her with a look of shocked
surprise. "You shameless hussy!" Louise shrieked
at her. "How dare you shout at me? You come into

my home like some common slut and try to take
away my husband. And right in front of my eyes
you try to carry on with him."

Sarah had already decided to confront the spirit
head on. "Chad is *my* husband now."

"What in tarnation do you mean, *your* husband?"

The spirit crossed the room and stood eye to
eye with her. Sarah could see the terrible hurt and
the anger churning within the spirit's aura.

Chad had been sitting on the edge of the bed
and was pulling off a boot when Sarah began
speaking to the invisible Louise. He sat there with
one hand on a boot heel—frozen, immobile, fearful lest some movement, some small sound, might
break the connection Sarah had established with
the other side.

In a firm, steady voice, Sarah told Louise she
was now in the spirit world. "You are no longer
a soul inhabiting a physical body. You are no
longer of the flesh. Remember the day you died.
Remember the day they buried you."

The tormented spirit put its hands to its ears.
"Stop it! Stop it! Or I'll scratch your eyes out!"

"You cannot harm me, Louise," Sarah told her.
"This house is no longer your home. The earth
plane is no longer your home. It is time for you
to pass on."

Louise's features became a mask of anguish. "I
cannot leave Chad. He still needs me."

"You need not worry about Chad," Sarah said
in a soft, soothing voice. "He's with me now. It
is time for you to pass on. You should have moved
on five years ago. You came together to complete

some karmic tie. You fulfilled your destiny together, and now it's time for Chad and me to work out our Karma."

Louise considered Sarah's counsel. "I know that Chad and I were meant to be together. I know that we had some lessons to learn together."

Sarah agreed. "And now Chad and I must walk together on the earth plane before we, too, pass to spirit. We, too, are meant to be together."

"But I will still worry so about him," the spirit protested.

"You need not worry about him," Sarah assured the spirit being. "The concerns of the earth plane should now mean nothing to you. Remember your loved ones with affection, but don't try to hang on to them. You must now be concerned only with things of the spirit."

Louise turned to look sadly at the confused rancher who sat on the edge of the bed. She began to weep. "I remember now. The minister standing over me. 'Ashes to ashes,' he said. All my relatives and friends were standing alongside him to agree.

"But I wasn't ready to leave. There was my husband to look after . . . and the ranch . . . and the hard times I knew were coming. I had to stick by Chad and help him. Two men came in white, shining suits and said that they would guide me, but I told them to go to blazes."

"Those men were your spirit helpers, your guardians," Sarah explained. "You should really have gone on with them. You should have realized that it was time for you to pass on."

"But I had to stay with my husband, don't you

understand?" Louise shouted, the anger within her flaring again. "And he rewards my fidelity by bringing you home with him from Saint Louis!"

Sarah did not flinch in the face of the spirit's rage. "He is my husband now, Louise. You have been in spirit for five years. It is not good that man should live alone."

"Alone?" Louise scowled. "He had me!"

"He had you while you were in your material body," Sarah said. "But you have been in spirit for five years."

"In spirit . . . five years?" Louise's spirit form began to vibrate in a peculiar manner.

Sensing that she had at last managed to help Louise to achieve some degree of comprehension of her true status in the greater reality, Sarah once again told the entity that she had been in spirit for five years.

Louise sighed and approached Chad. "That's why he has not touched me for these five long years. It was so unlike him to be so distant. He was always so affectionate. Then he just stopped touching me."

"Because," Sarah reminded her, "now you are in spirit."

"Now I am in spirit," Louise echoed.

Her image was beginning to waver. Realization of her actual state of existence was beginning to pervade her total energy pattern.

A brilliant, glowing orb formed behind Louise, and Sarah could perceive the forms of two angelic beings standing within the golden light.

"They're here again," Louise said. "Those same

two fellows are back again. The ones I told to go to blazes."

"Are you ready to go with them this time?" Sarah asked her.

Louise nodded. "Guess so. I have a greater understanding now. It's your turn to work out your own problems together. Just promise me that you'll be a good wife to him."

Before Sarah could reply, Louise stepped into the brilliant orb of golden, glowing light.

"I caught just a glimpse of two majestic figures in white," Sarah told me. "Behind them I saw a landscape of rich green grasses and multicolored flowers. Then there was nothing before me but my poor husband, still sitting on the edge of the bed, still holding on to his boot heel with one hand."

The spirit medium I have called Sarah Woodward eventually reentered the spiritualist ministry with the blessing of her husband. When she told me her story in 1973, she was nearly eighty years old and living in a nursing home in California— still alert, still studying, and writing down experiences taken from a lifetime spent fulfilling her destiny between two worlds.

Ten

He Married His Personal Prophet

The night was made for love. The snows had retreated from the Michigan countryside before the advance of spring; during the day, the sun placed a warm, friendly hand upon the backs of the winter-weary and drew them outside to fill their lungs with sweet country air. For a week or more the warm evening breezes had tossed the stars around, and the moon had glowed with a special magic that awakened the promise of renewal in the minds of all and had intensified the deepest longings in the hearts of young lovers.

James Galper, in the full flush of his twenty years, was excited beyond mortal words as, with the appreciation of a seasoned taster of fine wines, he let his eyes sip slowly at the face of the beauty next to him on the front seat of his car.

She wore her black hair long and straight, and her eyes were softly sad, reflecting depths of warmth and emotion. Her slender figure and long legs could have inspired the designer of the mini-skirt that she wore that night.

At last, James rediscovered his ability to form coherent thoughts and to speak.

"Bridget, I. . . ."

"Oh, thank you. I'm so glad that you think my hair looks lovely tonight, Jimmy. I washed it this afternoon, and I didn't really know if it would look good in time for the dance."

"Yeah, well, it looks fine. I was wondering. . . ."

"Why, Jimmy, you silly! Of course I had a wonderful time. I always have a good time with you."

James loosened his necktie. "Bridget is at it again," he thought. "I wonder if . . ."

"No way, Jimmy! I told you last time, none of that!"

James let out a deep sigh of resignation, then switched on the ignition. Carefully he guided his hardtop convertible out of the parking place by the river and back onto the main road.

"I'm glad," he dared to think, "that all the girls in Michigan aren't mind-readers!"

Today, nearly twenty years later, James Galper never tires of recounting anecdotes of those strangely romantic days when he was courting Bridget Muro, his "mindreader in a miniskirt."

"She always knew what I was thinking." He laughed. "How does a guy ever get ahead of a gal like that?"

"He never does, Jimmy," Bridget said with a winsome smile. "He never does. But I warned you that you were my destiny the first time we met at the municipal swimming pool."

James laughed even harder at that particular

memory. "I was nearly eighteen, going into my senior year in high school, and I was lifeguarding that summer at the pool. I really felt that I was Mr. Cool, getting paid for working on my tan and for eyeballing the knockout chicks in their scanty swimsuits. Then up walks this pretty little jailbait fifteen-year-old in a teeny-weeny red bikini and tells me that I am destined to marry her."

"And after he recovered from that shock, he found out more about me and really had his mind blown," Bridget said.

"Yeah, I found out that she was a sexy little witch who had even been written up in the local newspapers for her psychic powers."

"I prefer 'psychic abilities,'" Bridget said. Then she explained: "I've always been psychic. When I was thirteen, I found a lost three-year-old boy who had been missing in the woods for a couple of days. I wanted to remain anonymous—you know, just a psychic Good Samaritan—but the local papers got wind of it, the wire services and the tabloids picked up on it, and all of a sudden I was being confronted by total strangers who were begging me to heal them or make them rich."

"She became quite a local celebrity," James said, "but I had been too busy with football practice and my car and stuff, so I had missed her early notoriety."

I asked Bridget how, as a teenager, she had handled her abilities and her celebrity.

"There were times when I really enjoyed having these gifts from God, the Holy Spirit, the angels—wherever they came from," she said. "For example, I could read the boys like they were open books. Or I should say, open *Playboy* magazines. They would always get so flustered when I told them exactly what they were thinking. Then it got so none of the boys would date me, and hardly any of the girls wanted to be my friend. Those were the times I wished that some Higher Power would take my psychic abilities away from me."

How did her parents and other members of the family respond to her extrasensory talents?

"Mom liked it because I always knew what she was going to ask me beforehand, and I usually had the chore done even before she thought of it."

"Her dad and her brother Marty liked her abilities because they made a lot of money off her betting on sports events!"

Bridget seemed embarrassed by her husband's charge, but she didn't deny it. "I stopped giving them predictions, though. I'd always felt that there was something improper about using ESP to make money."

Intrigued by the lovely young psychic in the red bikini, James had begun dating Bridget. Although he sometimes became very frustrated and flustered by her extraordinary abilities, he learned to adjust to them and even to appreciate them.

"But then came the day when he didn't appreciate my abilities *enough,*" Bridget recalled. "And it almost cost us our lives."

Somewhat sheepishly, James agreed. They had dated through his senior year in high school, and they continued their relationship when he went off to college.

"I was home for the summer, working at my dad's supermarket," he said. "I was twenty going on twenty-one. Bridget was eighteen. It was a beautiful Sunday, and I said we should go on a real excursion and drive to Chicago, about five hours away. But Bridget had had this dream . . ."·

"I could remember the dream in very sharp detail," Bridget emphasized. "In my dream, Jimmy asked me to go riding with him into Illinois and on to Chicago. As we drove along the highway, we collided with another car, and both vehicles were badly damaged. Through drops of blood blurring my vision, I watched a woman with her arm bandaged and in a sling crawl out of the other car. I told Jimmy the dream and said we should definitely not drive out of town and out on the highway on that particular Sunday."

I asked James how he could have disobeyed Bridget's prophetic warning at this stage of their relationship. Surely the accuracy of her predictions had been proved time and time again.

He shook his head in wonder. "I don't believe it myself now, twenty years later," he admitted. "But you know, man, I kept saying to myself that it was just a *dream*. It wasn't like her usual predictions or her mind-reading. I mean, nearly every night you can see a lot of really nutty stuff in your dreams—thank the Lord they don't all come true!"

Bridget laughed. "He should have known that after all those years of having all these weird things happen to me, I *knew* the difference between a nutty dream and a prophetic one—but he just wouldn't listen."

"I wanted to see Chicago," was all James could offer in his defense.

"He coaxed and he begged and he pleaded with me to ride with him to Chicago," Bridget recalled with an exaggerated rolling of her eyes. "He kept asking me if I was going to let a silly dream interfere with an outing on such a gorgeous day. 'There won't be any wreck with old Steady Hand at the wheel,' he bragged."

Bridget's mother had been sitting on the front porch swing, reading the Sunday paper. "I think an automobile ride would be pleasant on such a fine day," she offered her opinion.

"Right on, Mrs. Muro," James had grinned, pleased to have her on his side. "And if we get started now, we can be back by just a little after midnight."

Against her better judgment and her psychic warning, Bridget finally yielded and followed the grinning James to his car.

"You drive carefully, Jimmy Galper," she admonished him, as she slid into the front seat.

And James did drive carefully—a point he has emphasized repeatedly—until they were halfway to Chicago. That was when they crashed into another car.

Bridget's head went through the windshield, and she staggered from James's automobile, wiping the blood out of her eyes.

"Dimly I saw the driver of the other car removing himself from behind the wheel with great effort," Bridget recalled. "The driver's wife was tugging at him with one good arm. Her other arm was bandaged and in a sling."

"While we sat in the emergency room, waiting to get Bridget's scalp stitched closed and my forehead bandaged, I kept begging her to forgive me for not listening to her dream warning," James said. "I said that I would never again doubt her predictions—especially when they concerned our welfare."

"And he never has," Bridget testified. "And Jimmy never again doubted that we were destined to be together."

James agreed. "And neither did I doubt her prediction that we would have three girls. I just started saving for their college fund."

Author Brad Steiger and his wife, Sherry Hansen Steiger, believe that marriage between Destined partners is the sacred path to understanding and spiritual growth. They work together to fulfill their mission of raising the spiritual level of planetary consciousness through their books, lectures, and seminars.

Ever since she was a teenager, Tara Buckland had in mind the precise image of the man that she would marry, and just how old she would be when they wed. She knew her husband would be English, a writer or artist, and that there would be a marked age difference between them. For over twelve years now, she has been married to Ray Buckland, the noted English author and teacher.

The acclaimed psychic-sensitive Clarisa Bernhardt had endured a number of tragedies of the heart and was beginning to despair of finding true happiness when Destiny brought a wonderful man named Norman into her life. Pictured here on their Canadian estate, one of their favorite racing horses, Pegasus Princess, can be seen in the background.

Stan Kalson, internationally known authority in the field of holistic health, learned from a friend's vision that a special woman would soon appear to serve as a helpmate in his work and in his life. When he developed a strong rapport with Lee Lage immediately after their first meeting, she confessed that his image had appeared to her in a meditation. They were truly Destined to be together.

When Dr. Lawrence Kennedy and Sandra Sitzmann first met, they went together like oil and water. Now, many years later, they have utilized the alchemy of love to transmute the ego issues and power struggles between two strong-willed people to form a solid and lasting relationship.

Patrick Flanagan and Gael Crystal Flanagan view their story of Destined love as a modern-day fairy tale. After being married in the Great Pyramid in Egypt, these "twin flames" have chosen to live in virtual seclusion, devoting their energies to the creation of scientific products and services to better humankind.

When her mother wanted to introduce her to an actor friend, Lisa's practical attorney instincts told her to avoid meeting another Hollywood "flake." However, this particular actor turned out to be John Hobson, a remarkable man who soon became the Knight in Shining Armor she had always yearned for.

David and Barbara Jungclaus have been led through many peaks and valleys in their spiritual evolution, but they have never lost their trust in Angelic Beings to see them through every challenge.

In show business since she was eleven, Laura Wesson thought she was immune to smooth-talking men with come-on lines. So she was more than skeptical of the fellow she'd just met who proclaimed his Destined love for her and said they had a past-life connection. Although she tried her best to resist, she learned that Destiny cannot be denied. Today, Laura and Dan Clausing conduct spiritual retreats at their Evening Star Ranch in Washington.

Eleven

Broadcasting on Destiny's Frequency

During a break between sessions when I was conducting an ESP seminar near Chicago in 1976, we began informally speaking about unusual things that various couples had done to spice up their relationships.

We had heard ideas such as feeding one another a meal using only fingers instead of utensils, leaving juicy love notes around the house in unexpected places, and wearing sexy lounging clothes to watch television.

Edgar, an attractive man in his early thirties, raised his hand and told of the time that he had rung their doorbell on Halloween. "And all I was wearing was a monster mask and a red jockstrap." He laughed at the memory. "And when Alice answered the doorbell, I yelled, 'Trick or treat, Baby!' She got so flustered, all she could say was, 'Where's your bag for the candy?'"

When the laughter from the seminar participants had died down, his wife added, "I think the neighbors were the ones who got the trick, looking at your bare bottom. I got the treat!"

Another time, according to Alice, Edgar had a grass skirt delivered to her office with a note telling her that he was preparing an exotic Hawaiian dinner at home and the only way she'd be admitted was if she was wearing the skirt and danced the hula.

"Edgar," I shook my head in mock wonder, "you have to be the Wizard of Wackiness and Marital Miracles to come up with these stunts to keep the sizzle in your marriage."

Alice, a full-figured redhead of seemingly perpetual cheerfulness, agreed. "He surely knows how to keep my fire glowing.

"One of my favorites was when he gave me a list before I left for work and asked me to pick up all the items he had written down before I came home. Well, it turned out to be a list for a sexy scavanger hunt. First, I went to a lingerie shop to pick up the nightie he'd bought for me. Then I went to the perfume section of a department store and got the bottles of perfume he'd reserved. And on and on, until I ended up at the liquor store to pick up the bottle of champagne that he had chilling.

"I arrived home to candlelight, soft music, a marvelous dinner, and the kids already at my mother's."

When everyone began to credit Edgar as the master of creating wild things to do to keep the spice in a marriage, he confessed that he had not always been Mr. Romantic, attuned to his lady love's needs and desires. He had, in fact, been a very self-centered and shallow young man—cold, emotionless, and intensely intellectual.

"I had to undergo a tough lesson about how we are all interconnected and how even our thoughts can affect the ones we love," Edgar said. "I had to find out for myself how it is possible to hurt the ones we love telepathically as well as emotionally."

Edgar Morris had always been a high academic achiever, and by the time he was a sophomore at a prestigious New England university, his classmates knew he raised the grading curve on any exam he took. For the academically oriented, Edgar Morris became *the* man to beat.

Near the end of his junior year, Edgar met Alice, and Cupid's deadly darts began to take a toll on his study time.

"The climax came after a big physics test," Edgar said. "When the grades were posted, I was mortified to see that I had received only an average mark. Some class members actually cheered, and nearly everyone was laughing at my humiliation. Later, one of my academic archrivals passed me in the corridor and whispered: 'Every Samson has his Delilah! I guess Alice is yours.' "

Edgar discovered to his embarrassment that he was not so academically aloof that he was immune to feeling the pinch of terrible pride.

"I went to a campus coffeehouse with Hank, my closest friend, and told him that I intended to break off with Alice," he recalled.

Hank was shocked. "Hey, c'mon, man. You

can't dump a great chick like Alice because of a little nick in the old grade points. You've got to be kidding."

Edgar said that he was deadly serious. "I can't jeopardize my academic standing. I really don't know what got into me, wasting all those hours spending time with that girl."

"You're unreal," Hank protested, shaking his head. "Alice is one foxy lady. You'd be nuts to drop her. Just study harder, man."

Edgar said that he most certainly intended to study harder, immediately, to make up his low mark in physics class.

"Perhaps one day I might take up with Alice again when things are back on an even keel," Edgar said firmly. "But as of this afternoon, at 3:55 P.M., Alice and I are no longer a 'thing.'"

"When are you going to tell her?" Hank asked. "Are you going to take her to dinner and announce your breakup for dessert? Send her a note by Express Mail? Or maybe make a curt telephone call? Maybe you just won't call her at all but instead will let her suffer, not knowing what goes on in that cold, sadistic, intellectual brain of yours."

"Thanks Hank, old friend," Edgar glowered. "You make me sound like a complete jerk."

"Anyone who'd dump a terrific girl like Alice because he didn't get his usual highest mark on a test is a complete, total, quintessential jerk!"

Edgar bade his friend farewell and went back to his room to attack the books with vigor. He would notify Alice of the change in their relationship in his own good time.

"After two or three days had passed," he said, "I began to notice that I had not seen Alice in the coffeehouse or in the one class we shared. When I inquired about her, I learned from one of her friends that Alice lay in a near-coma at the campus health service.

"According to her friend, Alice had been perfectly well and her usual exuberant self until about four o'clock three days before. She had suddenly heaved a deep sigh and fainted. Neither the girls nor the campus doctor had been able to revive Alice to full consciousness for more than short periods at a time."

Edgar went directly to the health service and asked to see her.

"I really felt awful that she was ill—and so mysteriously so," he said. "Although I had made a vow to break off with her, I had not yet seen her to tell her of my intentions. But then, neither had I called her for several days."

When he entered her room, Edgar saw that she was lying on the bed in what appeared to be a light state of trance sleep. She became immediately animated the moment he stepped into the room.

"You deceitful creep!" she screamed at him. "So I no longer mean anything to you! So you're going to break off with me! You cruel . . . cruel . . ."

Edgar was struck dumb with astonishment. How had she known of his intentions? Surely Hank would not have informed her.

"I heard your voice inside my head," Alice said, weeping her humiliation and sorrow. "I heard your voice saying that you wanted to dump me. And all because you got a lower-than-usual grade on a test! I can't believe you're so shallow. I can't believe you'd blame your errors on me. After all we've meant to each other. . . ."

"For a moment, Alice couldn't think of anything more to say, so I awkwardly, stupidly, childishly asked her what on earth she was talking about," Edgar said. "How could she have gotten such notions?"

Alice blew her nose, then sat up in bed and looked me straight in the eye. "I don't know how I heard you, but I heard your voice saying you intended to break up with me."

Edgar wanted to know when she had supposedly heard his voice uttering such a statement.

"It was around four o'clock, three days ago," she answered. "I had just gotten back from my class in child psychology."

"Somehow," Edgar said, "Alice had picked up my thoughts and words telepathically. I was immediately touched by the fact that our psyches had so merged that we had become as one mind. The universe suddenly became a very different place to me, and I realized that we truly must be responsible for every thought we think and every word we utter. I also realized how very much Alice meant to me and how callous I had been toward her.

"I really didn't know what to say or think, so I walked over to her bed and kissed her and told her that there was nothing to worry about. I loved her and I would spend the rest of my life showing her, rather than telling her, how much I cherished her presence in my life.

"Alice was out of the infirmary that next morning," Edgar said by way of conclusion, "and for fifteen years now I have honored my vow. I always find the necessary hours to spend with Alice, and neither my work nor the love of my life is ever neglected."

Telepathy often delivers cries for help between people who deeply love each other, as the following two stories show.

When Evelyn Romano experienced extreme feelings of uneasiness and nausea, she somehow knew that the uncomfortable sensations were related to her absent husband.

"Tony was at work," she said. "Although he had looked well when he had left for his job, I *knew* he was ill. It was as if I could actually hear him saying, 'Evelyn, please come and get me. I'm terribly sick.' And then awful waves of nausea would hit me."

Evelyn reached the point where she could no longer bear her uneasiness, and she changed her clothes and drove to the factory where her husband worked. Asking at the desk, she was told Tony was not at his job, but was in the dispensary.

When she walked into the dispensary, she found her husband sitting down, extremely pale and in great pain. The nurse on duty said she'd been trying to call Evelyn at home.

Two of Tony's co-workers stood on either side of him, ready to assist, if need be. Evelyn accepted their offer to help her husband into their car.

"Honey, what made you come after me?" Tony asked, once she had him home and in bed.

"I really don't know," she admitted. "I felt I was just being silly at first . . . or coming down with some bug myself. But it became increasingly clear to me that the terrible feeling of uneasiness was related to you and that you were sick and in pain."

"Well, sweetheart, you were certainly right," Tony sighed. "You came just when I needed you. You amazed everyone when you came walking into the dispensary while the nurse was trying to call you at home."

In the case of Shirley Nakashima, a telepathic call from her husband's hospital bed prompted her to take the action necessary to save his life.

"Nick had come down with a bad case of flu," she said. "I was staying at home with our children while he received medical attention in the hospital. I had just started to drift off to sleep that night when I clearly heard Nick's voice calling to me, 'Honey, I'm dying! Help me, help me! I'm dying but no one knows it!'"

Shirley didn't hesitate. She saw no need to attempt to rationalize the source of the voice. She knew that she had not been dreaming, and she knew that she had heard the voice of her husband.

It was after midnight when she arrived at the hospital.

"I was coldly informed that visiting hours were

over. Just as coldly, I insisted that they examine Nick," she said.

"Again, in a crisp, antiseptic manner, I was told that a night nurse had just looked in on my husband and that he was sleeping restfully. I was told that I should go home and leave the medical care of Nick to professionals."

Shirley would not be put off.

"I insisted that they call a doctor to examine Nick, or I would run into his room and look at him myself."

Shirley concedes that she is a rather small woman, but the nurses saw the determination in her eyes and could see that she meant exactly what she said. "My fierce look made me seven feet tall!"

The nurses summoned a doctor, who listened impatiently to Shirley's pleas.

"I know that it was just to humor me and to shut me up that he finally agreed to look in on Nick," Shirley said. "I waited at the desk for a few minutes, then I felt very strongly that my husband needed help immediately."

She brushed aside a nurse as she ran up the stairs toward Nick's room. "I heard the doctor say in a harsh whisper, 'Good Lord! This man is dying!'"

Quick work on the part of the doctor and the attending nurses saved Nick Nakashima's life.

Later, when he had regained consciousness, he told Shirley how he had lain there, knowing in the central core of his being that he was dying.

"I desperately sent a cry for help to you at home," Nick said. "We have always been so close, always knowing what the other would say before the words were spoken. I *knew* you would hear my thoughts and come to save me."

I am certain that many of us have known couples who have grown so close over the years that it is difficult to visualize one of them without the other. It may well be that such couples form an enormously powerful telepathic bond that becomes an integral element in their personal testament that they were destined to be together.

Highly respected experimental psychologist Dr. Stanley Krippner has expressed his opinion that the scientific establishment will soon have to revise its image of what it is to be human on the basis of telepathic evidence. At present, Dr. Krippner observes, psychology and psychiatry view each person as an entity separated from everyone else, as an alienated being.

"Telepathy," Dr. Krippner said, "may teach us that in the basic fabric of life, everything and everyone is linked, that man is continuously enmeshed, that he is always an integral part of all life on the face of the earth. So far, the scientific establishment has ignored this possibility; it will, for one thing, refute many of their basic concepts."

As the more than 20,000 respondents to our "Steiger Questionnaire of Mystical, Paranormal, and UFO Experiences" have testified, they are not at all respectful of the opposing dicta of scientific orthodoxy that decree that mental transmissions and receptions between humans are "impossible."

In fact, 90 percent of our respondents said that they had experienced at least one dramatic episode of telepathic communication. We are certain there are hundreds of thousands—if not millions—of men and women who have discovered through some profound telepathic link-up in their own lives that they are, indeed, "continuously enmeshed."

Thousands of laboratory tests have indicated a number of interesting facts concerning the conditions under which telepathy—and, in general, all testable psychic phenomena—work.

Distance appears to have no effect on telepathy or clairvoyance. Equally remarkable results have been achieved when the receiver was a yard away from the agent or when the experimenters were separated by many hundreds of miles. As Dr. S. G. Soal, a British researcher, has observed, "In telepathic communication, it is personality, or the linkage of personalities, that counts, not the spatial separation of bodies."

Attitude is of great importance in achieving successful telepathic communication. Cheerful, friendly folks almost always achieve better results in laboratory ESP tests.

It has also been demonstrated many times that those men and women who "believe" in their psychic abilities score consistently higher than skeptics and doubters.

Spontaneous psychic communication seems to work best under conditions that Dr. Jan Ehrenwald termed a "state of psychological inadequacy."

Naming this state of psychic readiness the "minus function," Dr. Ehrenwald believes that very often ". . . a necessary condition for telepathic functioning is a state of inadequacy or deficiency, such as loss or clouding of the consciousness," *i.e.,* sleep, hypnosis, trance, and so forth.

It is also fascinating to note that on the average, a man is more effective as the agent (the sender) and a woman is more effective as the receiver. This observation seems to apply to spontaneous instances of telepathy as well as to roles assumed under laboratory conditions. Other controlled experiments demonstrate that receivers often achieve better results if the agent is of the opposite sex.

All of which may be additional indications that such psychic abilities as telepathy are aspects of a fundamental and natural force that must be included in any total concept of humanhood and our world.

Twelve

A Karmic Love Bond

"Seriously, Brad," Diana Coronado told me, "it really is possible to die of a broken heart."

I nodded my agreement. "Yes, I am familiar with serious scientific research into so-called 'voodoo' deaths, or 'broken hearts.'"

Diana had entered my office in Scottsdale, Arizona, with her handkerchief already dabbing at her tear-rimmed brown eyes. She was weeping quite openly when she sat down. She had made an appointment to explore the possibility of a past life that might be impinging on her present life experience, but it appeared that she had another agenda she first needed to satisfy.

"There's a doctor who's done experiments with both humans and rats, and he's found an area in the brain that controls the heart," Diana informed me, after she had regained her composure.

"I believe it's called the 'insular cortex,'" I said.

Diana paid little attention to my interruption. "Well, this part of the brain is very sensitive to stress, and when it is stressed, it accelerates the beating of the heart. If this area, this insular cortex, should suffer extreme emotional stress, it can cause sudden death."

"So I've heard."

"So that's very likely what happens when someone dies for no apparent reason after they've lost a lover or a spouse through death or the sudden termination of a love affair," she said. "They've literally died of a broken heart."

"All right, Diana." I leaned back in my chair. "I appreciate your flying in all the way from Houston and paying my fee just to keep my files up to date on medical research."

She blinked in astonishment, completely missing the teasing nature of my remark. "I've come here to get your help so my heart doesn't break. I know that William and I must have some terrible karma to work out."

I knew Diana was no past-life groupie flying from one researcher to another. She was stylishly dressed, about thirty-five, and a businesswoman.

"I'll do my very best to see that you won't die of a broken heart, Diana," I promised.

Diana told me she'd been haunted by a recurring dream since early adolescence. In it, she saw herself dying of a fever in a crudely built cabin.

"I sense other people in the room, but my attention is riveted by a man who stands at the foot of my bed, looking down on me with extreme distaste. He seems somehow afraid of me, as though I have some dread disease he doesn't want to be exposed to. He turns his back to me and the others and walks out the door. Then I see flames crackling up around my bed.

"That's when I wake, screaming my terror and my sorrow," Diana said. "I feel the man was my husband. I know we lived in a crude cabin; before he deserted me, he set fire to the cabin to destroy both me and my disease."

Although she'd first had the disturbing dream when she was around eleven or twelve, Diana told me that she'd had an active adolescence and was not affected negatively by the vision.

"I firmly believed it to be a memory of a past life," she said. "I suppose I developed a healthy respect for fire and I was perhaps overly concerned about communicable diseases. I remember that I would go to great lengths to avoid contact with anyone who suffered a cold, but such an idiosyncrasy didn't cripple my social development."

Diana had married soon after graduation from college, and her union with Joseph Coronado produced two daughters, Beth and Lynn. Diana and Joe had legally separated nearly two years before. Numerous attempts at reconciliation had failed.

"I know our split was caused by my work," she said. "Joe wanted to marry Betty Homemaker. He didn't really believe I'd go back to work after Lynn was born. I know that he never believed I'd ever make more money than he did."

Seven months ago, Diana met William.

"He was getting off an elevator when I first saw him," she said. "His eyes seemed to pierce my very essence. I know that may sound like a purple passage from a romance novel, but I don't really care. I stood there as if I'd been turned to stone. Those were the eyes I had seen so often in my recurring dream. Those were the eyes of the husband who looked on me with revulsion and left me to die in a burning cabin."

Diana admitted that a strange rush of both love and hatred filled her trembling body. "I wanted to kiss him and strike him down at the same time. Somehow, I managed to push past him and get into the elevator."

When she returned to her office, she was shocked to find him waiting for her. "I know that I must have paled. I couldn't even manage to ask him his business. On the other hand, he seemed oblivious to my discomfort. He stood, flashed me a professional smile, and introduced himself as the new sales representative for one of our largest suppliers."

Diana remembered that she mumbled something that she hoped was reasonably appropriate, then sat down weakly behind her desk.

"When I began to calm down and gather some self-control, I wanted to laugh at the way Fate had reversed our positions," Diana said. "If I chose, I could cancel our order with that company and virtually destroy the man's career as a sales rep."

As they talked, she noticed William studying her. "I know this'll probably sound like a classic traveling salesman's line." He had grinned self-consciously. "But don't I know you from somewhere?"

"I think you probably do," Diana said frankly. For a moment, she thought she might blurt out the whole incredible story, but discretion prevailed.

"Are you originally from Houston?" he asked, seeking an answer. "We didn't go to college together, did we? I usually have such a good memory."

That might have been true, Diana mused, but did he have a memory that could stretch back a hundred years or more?

She accepted his invitation to dinner, and later, after several glasses of wine, she confronted him with her memory of his desertion and terrible deed in another lifetime.

William didn't run from the restaurant, shaking his head over his bizarre dinner with a lovely lunatic.

"He actually seemed contrite," Diana told me. "He listened to the account very attentively, and when I had concluded, he expressed his sorrow for having committed such a barbaric act."

I was skeptical. "Are you certain he hadn't had too much wine?"

Diana admitted freely that they had drunk a lot, but she denied that William could have been too drunk to follow the finer—and more startling—points of their conversation.

"Then you're telling me William believes in reincarnation?" I asked.

"He said he was open to the subject."

"So open that he didn't mind being called a vicious murdering swine over dinner? So open that he sat calmly through your accusations of betrayal and murder?"

"He said that while he couldn't imagine doing such a vile thing, he wanted to make reparation in this life," Diana said.

I could see that, in her mind, Diana was convinced she'd been reunited with William so he might work out his Karma and pay his debt to the Universe for his having deserted her in a prior life experience. She'd had the recurring dream to fortify her conviction.

I told Diana I was sorry, but I couldn't be certain William actually remembered a past life shared with her. He could be only a clever opportunist who sought to make his present life a bit more interesting.

"Not only does he have what to him may be nothing more than a flaky New Age excuse to have an affair with you," I pointed out quite bluntly, "it might cause you, as the buyer for the department store, to order larger shipments."

Diana's eyes misted over, and she reached once again for her handkerchief. "That's why I came to you, Brad. I wanted to be sure."

I was relieved to see that she was not that gullible. I reminded her that I was not a therapist.

"I know that." She nodded. "But I've read a number of your books, and I know that you do research with regressions into past lives. Besides, Joe has reentered the scene, and it seems as though a reconciliation might be possible. I want you to regress me so that I might determine which man is truly my destiny—William or Joseph."

I was willing to attempt a past-life exploration with her, but I stressed that any life-altering decision derived from the experience would be totally of her own volition.

While there are few tales more romantic than those of reincarnated lovers who have once again

managed to find each other over the span of
centuries, caution must be exercised so we
don't fall into the trap of believing that every
person who projects physical attractiveness or
sex appeal to us indicates a past-life relationship between us.

I have conducted many regressions for people
with marital maladjustment, emotional entangle-
ments, and sexual traumas. Many obtained a re-
lease of present life phobias by reliving the origin
of their trauma in some alleged former existence.
I found it extremely effective to focus on the particular past life that I call the Karmic Counterpart,
that former existence that appears to be directly
responsible for the troublesome imbalance and/or
confusion in the subject's present life experience.
In many cases, we needed only one session to enable the person to see that he or she had been
unknowingly allowing unconscious memories of a
prior existence to threaten or to ruin a fruitful relationship or a productive existence in the present
life experience. I decided I would use the Karmic
Counterpart technique with Diana.

I used a relaxation technique to place Diana in
a deeply altered state of consciousness.

Once she was as relaxed as possible, I called
upon the real Diana within to become aware of a
beautiful figure robed in violet standing near her
tranquil, resting physical body. This beautiful figure, I told Diana, was her spiritual guide, her
guardian angel, who would take the *Real Diana*
out of her physical shell and travel with her to a

higher dimension where she would be able to receive knowledge of a past life that she needed to know about—a past life that had greatly influenced her present life experience.

This particular past life, I told the entranced Diana, would be one in which she would see a good many individuals who had come with her to her present life experience to complete a task left unfinished, to learn a lesson left unaccomplished. *Whatever* she saw, I stressed, would be for her good and for her gaining. She had nothing to fear, I reassured her, for her guardian angel would be ever near, allowing nothing to harm her.

I moved Diana back in time and space to the past life that was primarily responsible for her present life experience. I instructed her to see the reasons why her soul chose the parents, the brothers or sisters, the friends, the lovers, the nationality, the race, the sex, the talents, the occupation that she had, and to see the soul-chosen purpose for the agonies, troubles, pains, and griefs that had entered her life.

When I asked her to speak and to identify where she was in terms of country and year, Diana said that she *felt* she was in Georgia, in about the year 1850.

Brad: What sex are you?

Diana: Female.

Brad: As you view yourself now, how old are you? And please describe yourself.

Diana: I'm in my late thirties, maybe forty. I am not too tall, and I have dark brown hair streaked with gray. I have blue eyes.

Brad: What is your name in that lifetime?

Diana: Magdalena . . . Magdalena Esta . . . Maybe Estabrook . . . Esterbrook. My back hurts.

Brad: Why does your back hurt? Go deep into the memory. *Be* Magdalena once again. Feel what she felt; know what she knew.

Diana: I've been carrying heavy pails of water in the slave quarters and lifting the coloreds who are too weak and helping them to get into their beds.

Brad: Why are you doing this?

Diana: There's some kind of terrible plague that is sweeping over the plantations here in Georgia. It's been striking down both fieldhands and house slaves. I'm doing my best to care for them . . . to help them get well. A lot of them are dying. A lot of white folks are dying, too. I'm doing my best to nurse them.

Brad: That must be a big job. No wonder your back hurts. Isn't there anyone to help you? What about your husband?

Diana: Arthur was working alongside me until he took sick. Most of our neighbors say that they're just slaves. They say we're damn fools to take any chance of catching the plague. Just let 'em die and burn the bodies. But me and Arthur believe that they're people, too. And we believe it's our Christian duty and our responsibility to look after them and care for them. Naomi, one of the house slaves, and Benjamin, her husband, been working right beside me day and night ever since Arthur collapsed.

I asked Diana to go even deeper into her past-life memory and to see if any one of those people—her husband, Naomi, or Benjamin—had come with her to her present life experience. Her features assumed an expression of shock and surprise.

"Arthur . . . he's my husband Joseph!" she gasped. "I can't believe it. And . . . and Naomi . . . she's Beth. And Lynn, my goodness to glory, she was Benjamin."

Tears were running unchecked over Diana's cheeks. Once a subject has been placed in an altered state of consciousness and regressed to a prior life experience, things don't always turn out the way the subject expected. I knew that prior to my placing her in a hypnotic state, Diana had believed William had been her past-life husband.

I told Diana to move ahead in that time one week.

Diana: I'm sick! Oh, Lordy, I am sick!

Brad: Did you catch the plague?

Diana: Dear God, I must have. I am really sick . . . I . . . can't talk . . .

I instructed her that all pain, distress, and agony would be taken from her and she would be able to speak freely.

Diana: Arthur . . . I think Arthur is dead. We're in one of the slave cabins. I was nursing Hannibal and his wife and child when I just keeled over. Hannibal, bless his heart, let me lie down in his bed. I . . . I'm too weak to move.

I inquired about Naomi and Benjamin.

Diana: Benjamin is either dead or dying; I don't know which. Naomi is here with me. She's still strong. No plague gonna be able to get her. Hey, there's someone coming!

Brad: Someone coming to help you?

Diana: I should say not. It's our overseer, Mr.

Napier, he's got a torch in his hand. He's cursing
Arthur and me for being such fools. He says we
gave our lives for nothing . . . for trying to help
a bunch of slaves.

Brad: What's he doing with the torch?

Diana: He's says he's going to burn down the
slave quarters. That's the only way to get rid of
the plague on the plantation. He says he's gonna
burn us along with it. He's looking at me with
such contempt and disgust. Then he sets fire to
the cabin! He's going to burn me alive! Naomi
tries to beat out the fire with her feet and hands
and a blanket. Mr. Napier clubs her down with
the butt of his shotgun. He hits her until she lies
still. Flames are all around me now . . ."

I moved Diana ahead until she was past her
death agony. When she said that her spirit was
floating above the scene of fiery destruction and
she felt unemotional and detached from the terrible events below, I told her she'd be able to see
clearly Mr. Napier had come with her to her present life experience.

Diana: It's William. I knew him by the eyes.
It's been those cruel eyes looking at me with distaste and disgust that have haunted me all my life.

Before I brought Diana back to the present, I
told her that her angel guide would allow her to
receive any lesson or teaching that she should
know for her good.

"My spiritual guide showed me that Joseph had
felt insecure when I'd received a promotion," she
said. "This triggered his past-life memory of the

life in which I took it upon myself to attempt to care for the victims of the plague. I had asserted myself more than the average woman of that time period, and I had paid for my independent action with my life. Somehow, he had become insecure and frightened that my rising above the crowd, so to speak, would once again cause my destruction. These fears led to the senseless arguments that brought about our separation."

How did she feel now about her unresolved karma with William?

"I'm going to keep him at arm's length and maintain our relationship at a professional level," she answered without hesitation. "He has yet to receive any kind of noticeable level of higher awareness. Perhaps, slowly, I can help him raise his consciousness.

"I can see clearly now that Joe really is my destiny. I know now that we were brought together in our present lives to continue our love bond. Thank you, Brad, for not allowing me to die of a broken heart!"

Thirteen

The Romantic Mystery of Soulmates

When I met Bix Carter in 1977, he was in his early sixties and internationally recognized for his ability to blend aspects of traditional African art with contemporary surrealistic expression. We had become friends, and whenever I was in San Francisco, I tried to make time to visit the combination studio and apartment he shared with his third wife, Lois, an author of children's books. One night after I had lectured at a metaphysical conference, a group of us followed Bix and Lois back to their place.

"Brad, you were so correct during the question-and-answer period when you cautioned that young woman about pursuing the man she believed to be her soulmate," Alisha, an astrologer, said to me, as we talked over wine and sliced apples and cheese. "Unless they were fated to be together again in this life, she could truly be opening herself up to a lot of heartache."

I was pleased with her agreement. "I always caution people about the soulmate concept. So many unscrupulous Don Juan types use the old 'You are my soulmate' or 'We must have been lovers in a past life' lines just to chalk up another sexual conquest."

Sandy, a past-life reader from the Bay area, asked, "But you *do* believe in soulmates, don't you, Brad?"

"Yes, I believe we may come together with our 'other half,' in many lifetimes, for the growth of our souls. I just think we should be more judicious in awarding the title. I know some metaphysicians who seem to have a 'soulmate of the month.'"

Alisha laughed at my observation along with the others, then shook her head in sad reflection. "You're right. Too many guys and gals in the New Age field use the old soulmate line as a justification for their current love affair."

Bix Carter laughed. "That is so disgustingly true," he said. "Yet no tale is quite so romantic as that of two lovers who have found each other again after a past lifetime of love."

He reached inside his coat pocket and withdrew his wallet. "I recognized Lois as my soulmate the moment I saw her," he said, handing me a photograph.

The photograph was of a very young girl standing at a ship's railing. Just to her side was an older woman. The picture was very wrinkled and had been pressed between adhesive plastic sheets to preserve it. At first I thought that it might be a snapshot of one of their daughters, but the picture was too old, older than either of their teenaged girls. Judging from the older woman's dress,

I guessed the picture had been taken sometime in the forties.

"That's a picture of Lois when she was nine," Bix said, after we had studied the photograph. "I took that picture the first time I set eyes on her because I recognized her immediately as my soulmate."

Everyone knew Bix was a couple of decades older than his wife, so a lot of silent arithmetic was going on inside a lot of heads.

"I really was nine years old in that photograph," Lois smiled affirmation. "Bix took that picture in 1940, when my family traveled by boat to Hawaii."

"I was going on twenty-seven," Bix said. "I had already knocked around the country for quite a few years when I got a job as a merchant seaman sailing out of San Francisco."

Alisha's eyes were wide with amazement. "And you, as a grown man of twenty-seven, took one look at this nine-year-old girl—and *knew* she was your soulmate?"

Bix nodded. "I was getting ready to load some cargo into the hold when I happened to glance toward the gangplank and see a family of five coming on board—husband, wife, two young boys, one little girl. When I saw that little girl, it was as if she was suddenly bathed in a bright, golden light—and I knew that I had rediscovered my soulmate."

Sandy could not suppress a giggle. "That's all well and good, Bix, but what did you do with such knowledge? You surely didn't run up and try to hit on a nine-year-old! There are laws against such things."

The man who had accompanied Sandy agreed. "She was even younger than Lolita," he scolded Bix in mock seriousness. "Bad form."

Bix shrugged his broad shoulders. "Obviously, I didn't want to be thrown overboard and fed to the sharks as a pervert. So I did nothing. Nothing, that is, except take this picture one sunny afternoon."

Bix is a natural storyteller who loves to play to an audience. It didn't take any coaxing to get him to tell us the story of their second meeting.

Two weeks after the United States entered the war in December 1941, Bix enlisted in the army. He was wounded in 1944 during heavy fighting in Italy and sent back to the States.

"After my discharge in '45, I started painting. I had experienced a series of visions while I was in the hospital that showed me how I could use my African roots in new and exciting ways. I had my first one-man show in New York in 1950, then moved back to San Francisco."

Lois was the daughter of teachers who had accepted positions in the Honolulu school system. Although her parents looked upon the job in Oahu as a temporary change of scene before a return to the mainland, the attack on Pearl Harbor altered their plans significantly.

"We became permanent residents," she said. "My parents and one of my brothers still live on the big island of Hawaii. I returned to the mainland to attend Berkeley in 1950. I wanted to be a professional painter, but I knew I wasn't good enough to be more than a weekend dabbler. I decided to write about the arts and contemporary culture instead."

In 1965, Lois was given an assignment by a national magazine to interview Bix Carter.

"By that time," Bix chuckled, "I had gone through two wives who seemed dedicated to the proposition that my life should be a living hell on earth. I was not looking for romance, believe me. I had decided to devote all my energies to my painting. But when Lois walked into my studio, I swear to God that I recognized her at once. I was fifty-two . . . she was thirty-four . . . but I knew exactly who she was. She was my soulmate. And that same bright golden glow was all around her!"

Lois had arrived at his studio and nervously approached the celebrated painter with the tentative preamble: "I hear you're easy to talk with."

Bix laughed at the memory and gave his wife an affectionate squeeze. "I said, 'Sister, I've got a whole lot of talking to do with you. I've been waiting for you to walk through my door for twenty-five years!'"

Lois reached up and kissed her husband's cheek. "I thought it was some corny line until he reached in his pocket and dug out that picture."

Sandy wanted to know if Lois had recognized herself in the old photo.

"Of course I did," Lois said. "But I wanted to know how the hell he had been able to get into our family scrapbooks."

When Bix had explained and told her the entire story of his twenty-five years of waiting for her

to reappear in his life, she was so stunned she
postponed the interview for a couple of days.

"That night, I experienced a powerful past-life
dream that identified Bix as my husband in ancient Greece. It was an idyllic life experience,
filled with love and intimacy. I woke up crying,
and I could hardly wait to return to Bix's studio.
Later, during a regression, we both recalled other
past lives in Egypt and Peru. We really were born
again to be together!"

Someone asked why there had been such a dis-
parity in their ages in their present life experience
and why it had taken them so long to be reunited.

"I don't think anyone has the answers to those
kinds of questions," Bix said. "The important
thing is that we did find each other somewhere
along the way and that we are privileged to journey on our earthwalk together just as long as we
can."

There can be no question in anyone's mind that
Bix and Lois Carter are destined lovers and that
they truly are soulmates. But not all soulmate re-
unions are as smoothly accomplished. Witness the
following account from a well-known professional
educator:

> I met my twin spirit in 1959. I knew in an
> instant that I had known him for 10,000
> years. At that time I had no knowledge what-
> soever of psychic matters—nor did I know
> anything of twin spirits. I simply felt a pull

so strong that I was overwhelmed. He was a teacher and I was his student.

After the initial meeting, we did not see each other for several years. But he was brought back into my life at least two dozen times for extended periods of time. We have worked together, have traveled the world together, and are aware of our twin spirit relationship. However, even though there are pleasant memories, the relationship has been a tortured one as well.

My soulmate, a brilliant academic, does not have a high enough level of awareness to pursue our twin spirit relationship to its zenith. Our energy together is so strong that it frightens him—and he must back away from it whenever he can to recover. I have tried through the years to raise his level of awareness—and have succeeded to a great degree.

About four years ago, I decided never to see him again. It was just too painful for me. But we are working together again in very close proximity on a number of important projects. My family and friends are afraid because along with his support through thirty-three years, there has also been betrayal.

We are completely telepathic. I can "pick him up" regardless of where in the world he is. This telepathy has caused us problems because I think he has said something aloud when he has only thought it.

Our relationship has torn me up, but I finally learned to live with it—by continuing to love him, but breaking the attachment to his karmic destiny. By doing that, I no longer anguish when we are not together—nor do I have dreams of what could be or what might have been.

I have no idea what the future holds for us. Perhaps we'll only remain friends in this lifetime. The universe works in strange ways, and I can't predict what might happen.

I'm really happy that I met my twin spirit, because I know what it feels like to be truly happy with the opposite sex. I also know what it's like to have my soul energy multiplied by ten so that I feel like I'm soaring when we are together. My life has changed enormously since I met my soulmate three decades ago—and over all, it has been a fortuitous encounter.

My friend Benjamin Smith is also one who knows that he met and married his soulmate—but it was not ordained that they should stay together in this lifetime. Ben told me their story:

I first met Nancy when I was president of a service club and was interviewed by her on a local television station in Eugene, Oregon. I fell in love with her on that day, but I didn't follow up on my feelings because she was wearing a wedding ring (even though I found out later that she wasn't married at the time). I admired her from afar, and I went through another marriage before I asked her out.

On our first date, we had an almost instant bonding, and we stayed up until 5 A.M. just talking . . . within four months we were living together, and we were married the following March. It had been ten years from the first time I'd met and fallen in love with her until I married my soulmate.

I believe a soulmate is someone with whom you have built up a karmic bond over several lifetimes. Upon investigation, Nancy and I discovered that we had spent at least seven lifetimes together.

We were able to communicate without speaking. Once we went on a two-hour drive and spoke perhaps a dozen words out loud— but we held an intensely deep conversation for the entire drive. Many times I would know what she wanted or what she was going to say before she uttered a word.

Ours wasn't necessarily the happiest of relationships, but it was the deepest love I have ever felt—and the most complete psychic connection I have experienced. I learned a great deal in the relationship, and I'm certain she did as well. We explored metaphysics together, and we joined a group of fellow explorers who met weekly for several years.

I knew a year before she did that we had to go our separate ways. We had completed what we had come together to do. But I also knew that she was the one who had to make the split. I had left her in previous lifetimes and I couldn't do it this time around.

Our marriage lasted ten years—and our friendship still endures. She has remarried and lives in the Southeast, but we still correspond; and I know that if I really needed her, she would be there for me—and I for her. We became close enough that we lived together in the same house for about a year after the divorce became final.

I still love Nancy a great deal, even though I know that we've completed what we needed to do in this lifetime and that we had to go different directions. Someday I know that we will be together again, but not in this lifetime—and perhaps not even on this level of knowing.

Fourteen

The Universe Brought Him to Her

Clarisa Bernhardt is the only psychic-sensitive in modern times to predict an earthquake to the day, the location, the magnitude—and even the minute. The astonishing documented prediction was made on her radio show *Exploration* and referred exactly to the 1974 Thanksgiving Day quake in San Jose, California.

Although the attractive blonde bears the oft-bestowed title of "Earthquake Lady" with a tolerant smile, her paranormal talents are not limited to quake predictions. She has demonstrated an additional use of ESP by locating lost people and by cooperating with law enforcement agencies as a psychic sleuth. She is regularly consulted by business executives who seek her assistance in making top-level decisions, and she is an extremely gifted medium.

I first became acquainted with Clarisa in 1973, when I was researching my book *Medicine Power: The American Indian's Revival of His Spiritual Heritage and Its Relevance for Modern Man*

(Doubleday, 1974). Clarisa, who is half Cherokee, the granddaughter of Chief John Muskrat of Tahlequah, Oklahoma, told me of her experience in a haunted California ranchhouse with the ghost of a Shumash chief who liked to greet guests with a hotfoot.

As one of the spirit's victims put it, "You'll believe it for yourself after he comes into the room while you're in bed and burns your foot. Then nobody will believe *you!*"

Clarisa's friend Flo owned the house but had not experienced any unusual spirit phenomena until after she'd remodeled the place—then no one could spend the night there without waking up with red marks on fingers or toes and without experiencing burning sensations.

"The house had been built over a Shumash graveyard," Clarisa recalled. "You could feel a presence in that house as soon as you entered. Since I have the spiritual privilege of seeing people on the other plane, I met the chief in the hallway, where there was a very high vibration. The Shumash were apparently a very evolved people. At first the spirit was hostile to me, but after a couple of visits, he was all right."

I had grieved with Clarisa when she'd lost her husband, Russ; and I had commiserated with her when she'd later found herself in an unproductive and negative relationship. I could not have been happier when she met and married Norman, her present husband.

"He's a wonderful human being and a very spiritual man," she said. "It's been a great blessing in my life that the universe brought me Norman, and I'm thankful for the events that occurred at just the right time in my life to allow me to make the right decisions. You and Sherry know that it's important to be with a person who's spiritual, as well as interested in worldly things, who treats you well, and who professes to be in love with you."

Clarisa said that the manner in which she first met Norman and the strange way they got together was like something right out of a novel.

In the summer of 1984, Clarisa's good friends, the scientists Patrick and Gael Crystal Flanagan invited her to present a lecture on "Earthquake Predictions and Visions" at a one-day seminar they were hosting in Scottsdale, Arizona.

After she'd completed her presentation and had instructed audience members on how they might apply the sixth sense in a practical way in everyday life, Clarisa noticed one man standing back from the others crowding around her for the opportunity to speak with her personally. She could not help noticing him, for he had an extremely brilliant auric field surrounding him. Since childhood, Clarisa has had the ability to perceive the human aura, the magnetic field every individual possesses.

"As he walked toward me," she recalled, "I thought he had the most engaging smile, and he looked as though he'd just stepped out of a men's fashion magazine. He was very handsome and very magnetic."

He introduced himself as Norman, a Canadian from Winnipeg, and he requested a psychic reading. He explained that he was short on time, as he had to catch a plane to Mexico early the next morning.

Later that afternoon, they met outside the conference room, and Clarisa attuned herself to receive the answers to his many questions.

As he rose to leave, he looked at her very intently and asked a final question: "Do you feel I'll ever meet someone very special in my life?"

Clarisa took a deep breath and gazed steadily into Norman's aura. "As I continued to gaze, a figure began to become visible. The features became very clear. In fact, it was like looking into a mirror!"

She could not suppress a sudden gasp of surprise. It couldn't be! But the image in her vision was . . . *her own!*

"Is something wrong?" Norman wanted to know.

"Oh, no, nothing at all," Clarisa said, trying desperately to regain her composure. "I . . . I see that . . . in the next twelve months, approximately, you will definitely meet this person."

"But how will I know her?" Norman asked, wanting to be certain he didn't miss his golden opportunity.

Clarisa was in a quandary. She certainly was not going to give Norman a description of herself.

"Oh, you'll know her," Clarisa finally answered, hoping a general reply would suffice. "Just follow your heart."

"But what does she look like?" Norman persisted.

Clarisa hesitated, praying for the right words to

come out of her mouth. "Well, she's sort of blondish."

Clarisa is very blond and she didn't want to push her own image on Norman. "But . . . maybe more of a sandy blonde . . . a sandy blonde leaning to a darker blonde . . . sometimes bordering on a light brown. Yes, that's it . . . light brown."

Norman smiled. "Sounds good," he said, as he walked away.

All that day Clarisa remained baffled by the unusual experience. Why had she seen herself in this stranger's aura? Certainly he had an extraordinarily positive vibration around him, but he had struck a most peculiar chord in her heart, as if he were someone very special to her.

She had always believed in maintaining a professional and impersonal attitude toward her clients. She had been nothing but professional with Norman, but she had never felt like this before. She had made it a point never to allow her personal feelings to cause any distraction from her work.

Perhaps she needed to take a vacation. She had to admit that she had been under stress because of an unhappy personal relationship. She had been too vulnerable during a period when she was recovering from the loss of her late husband.

"I became aware that it was a beautiful day in Scottsdale. As I rose from the area where I had given Norman his reading and placed various papers in my briefcase, I decided it had been very nice to meet him, and I hoped all good things happened for him. We were worlds apart. There was no advantage to be wasting time with 'what ifs,' so I flew back to California."

In the months to follow, Clarisa was surprised to receive a couple of telephone calls from Norman. She was delighted to hear that he was pleased with the information and guidance she'd given him on several of his projects. He also arranged a telephone consultation with her for additional psychic guidance. Before he ended the call, he told her he'd missed seeing her at another conference in Scottsdale.

In August 1985, she experienced a vivid dream of being in an elegant airplane. She was seated on the aisle, and when a voice announced, "You are to change now," she immediately got up and was ushered into an extravagantly decorated section of the craft. Just as she was settling into the harmony and comfort of the plush environment, the plane suddenly encountered turbulance—and she awakened.

She knew the dream had to be symbolic, and she was certainly going through a period of turbulance in her personal life. Feeling too off balance to be objective enough to use her own psychic talents, she called her friend Gael Crystal Flanagan.

"Gael, who has her own special brand of spiritual magic, said I should come to visit them in Arizona. Then she asked if I remembered Norman."

Gael told Clarisa that Norman had asked about her when he'd attended the Flanagans' conference that summer.

"He said he found you fascinating," Gael continued, "and if you hadn't been involved in a relationship, he'd have liked to have had the opportunity to get to know you better. He even went so far as to say that under the right circumstances, he felt he could easily fall in love with you."

Clarisa listened to Gael without saying a word. She remembered how nice Norman had seemed.

She was startled to hear Gael telling her to stay by the phone. "I'm making a call, and I'll get back to you."

"Gael," she protested, "you're not calling Norman?"

The telephone line only buzzed at her. Gael had hung up.

Twenty minutes later, Clarisa answered the phone to hear Norman's voice.

"Although I was a bit embarrassed," Clarisa admitted, "his openness and his charm quickly put me at ease. Norman said I should come to Canada to visit him for a few days—no strings attached. The vibrations felt very good again. I accepted Norman's invitation; in less than forty-eight hours, I was on the plane flying to Canada—and into the most wonderful and romantic adventure of my life. And it continues to this day, ten years later!"

Before Clarisa's visit ended, she and Norman decided they wanted to be together to see how things would work out.

"We traveled to Arizona for the winter, first visiting the area in Scottsdale where we'd first met, then spending five marvelous months in Sedona.

"When we arrived in Sedona, we stayed for a few days at the lovely Phantom Ranch, atop the mesa near the airport. We were so pleased when

Gael and Patrick arranged to meet us for an afternoon. Gael brought us a gift of some crystals she had taken with them on their wedding night in the great Pyramid at Giza.

"That night, in meditation, I received a beautiful vision of having known and loved Norman in many lifetimes, including one in Egypt and another when we were students in an ancient Aztec pyramid.

"I am so thankful that Norman and I were able to meet in this lifetime and to be together," Clarisa said. "He has been a great inspiration to me. There has been an incredible magic between us . . . and it continues!"

Fifteen

Two Souls Reconnect

Those who have read *Angels of Love* will recall that it was at an event sponsored by my friend Stan Kalson that I encountered the lovely blonde, Mary Caroline Meadows, whose physical body was temporarily usurped by an angelic being to see that I got together with Sherry Hansen. When Stan wrote to tell me how much he loved the book *Angels of Love,* I asked if he'd consider sharing his own story of how he reconnected with his past-life love, Lee Lagé.

When Stan and I first met in 1977, he was already recognized as an authority in the field of holistic health, and soon after our meeting he traveled worldwide, teaching concepts of nutrition and energy healing.

After a few years of using Phoenix, Arizona, as a base, Stan became undecided as to whether he should stay in Phoenix to continue his networking activities or return to Honolulu. He remembered the decision as a truly tough one.

"I attended the Human Unity Conference in

Vancouver, British Columbia, and received the inspiration to start a holistic resource, the *Arizona Networking News,*" he said. "When I returned to Phoenix, I needed a place to live, an automobile, and individuals to support my new brainchild. I boldly stated that if all these things did not manifest quickly, I would gladly return to Honolulu."

Finding an automobile was easy, and new living quarters were found through an ad in the newspaper. When John Cheney, the owner of the house for rent, opened his door, he took one look at Stan and asked, "Have we met each other before?"

"Later, as we visited at greater length, we both realized we'd never met before that evening. I inquired about John's occupation. He was a graphic artist. The Angels of Love were working quickly to keep me in Phoenix to meet my past-life love."

She, however, did not arrive immediately.

"I obviously had more lessons to learn as I sought to develop the *Arizona Networking News.* For the first three issues, I did most of the work, struggling to the point of exhaustion. I was feeling largely unsupported by most of the others involved in the project."

At this time, Stan received a letter from Vince Halpin, whom he'd met briefly while on tour in Australia. Vince wrote that he'd be in Phoenix and would like to spend some time with Stan.

"Upon Vince's arrival, I discovered that he was a devotee of Paramahansa Yogananda. The Self Realization Fellowship had been my spiritual refuge. Although I had never formally studied their teachings, I had always felt spiritually connected to Yogananda."

When they visited the temple of the Self Realization Fellowship in Phoenix, Stan opened his eyes during a meditation and noticed that a particular photograph of Yogananda seemed alive.

"Especially his eyes," Stan recalled. "I kept opening and closing my eyes to see if my observation would change, but it stayed the same."

After an hour of meditation, Stan nudged Vince to indicate that he was ready to go.

As they were leaving the temple, Vince said that Yogananda had spoken and given him a message for Stan.

"For me?" Stan asked, quite surprised.

"Yes," Vince replied. "He is sending a special woman to you who will join you in your work and life."

Stan smiled, thanked him for the message—and quickly dismissed it.

"Shortly after Vince had left Phoenix to return home, I was invited to discuss holistic health concepts on the radio," Stan said. "The interviewer was unprepared, and we did not have a good rapport. Once before, he had scheduled an interview with me—and he had not even shown up at the studio to conduct it. He had never offered a word of explanation or apology. Patiently, I sought to create a positive situation out of a negative one, and I guided the interviewer through one very *long* hour. Later, I wondered why I'd ever agreed to do the interview."

Two weeks after the awkward radio interview, the announcer left the radio station to work at a public relations firm for which Lee Lagé produced health-oriented radio programs. One day she an-

nounced out loud that she needed a guest who
was well-informed about holistic concepts for one
of her health shows.

The former radio host said that he knew someone. "But look out," he warned. "This Kalson
guy will try to take charge of the interview."

Somewhat reluctantly, Lee called Stan and arranged a time for him to be interviewed. Stan
liked her pleasant voice and agreed to do the radio
program.

"The day of the scheduled interview had been
a terribly busy and hectic one for me," Stan remembered. "In order to help reduce stress, I was
hanging upside down on a gravity inversion machine when I realized the live radio show on
which I'd agreed to appear would begin in twenty
minutes!"

Stan dashed out the door unshaven and dressed
only in T-shirt, shorts, and sandals, and he arrived
at the studio with only seconds to spare.

Nervous and stressed because she feared her
guest was about to become a no-show, a relieved
but disoriented Lee Lagé introduced their guest
authority as Stan *Kalston* and the interview began.

"The interview proceeded without my being in
my body!" Stan emphasized. "To this day I do
not know what I said. However, the host loved the
interview—and Lee followed me to my car."

Both Stan and Lee felt a wonderful rapport and
a strong attraction to each other, as if they had
known one another for a long time.

After they had talked for a time, Lee told Stan
she was a member of Self Realization Fellowship

and that his image had once appeared in her meditation so strongly that she had waited for him at
the door.

While Stan had not appeared physically at the
temple for Lee on that occasion, he had manifested for her that afternoon at the radio studio.

"Lee's confession definitely excited me," Stan
admitted, "and I began to think that she must be
the special woman Paramahansa Yogananda was
sending me."

The two parted that day, not yet comprehending
the bigger plan for their spiritual love connection.
Lee recalled that she returned to her office and
told all the secretaries that she and Stan Kalson
would soon be living and working together.

"You just met him!" they all screamed at her.

"Never mind that!" she told them. "It *will* happen."

That evening she told her best friend, Georgia
Ross, all the details of her meeting Stan Kalson.

Georgia screamed out, "That's who I've been
telling you about! How many times have I told
you the two of you should meet? I just knew the
two of you would like each other."

It all came back to Lee. "I put that name completely out of mind," she laughed. "I remember
now your mentioning your meeting Stan, but I
thought you said he was married, so I just mentally erased his name."

Not long after their initial meeting, Stan and
Lee began to date and to develop deep feelings
for one another. Stan wanted her to work with him
on the newspaper and to become a part of the

International Holistic Center. Lee did not want to leave the security of her public relations job.

One night Georgia, Lee, and a few other friends went to a nightclub that featured Richard Ireland, a most remarkable psychic of wide reputation.

Blindfolded, Ireland placed slips of paper with questions from the audience up to his forehead. "Is there a Lee Lagé present here tonight?" he asked.

Startled, Lee managed to answer, "Here I am!"

As he held her folded paper to his forehead, he said aloud: "The question is, 'Where will I be working?' "

Lee could hardly contain her amazement. "That's right. That's my question."

"Yes, I see that you will change jobs. I see that you will be working with Stan Kalson of the International Holistic Center!"

Lee screamed her wonderment—and so did the rest of her friends.

Lee did work with Stan, and for many years they coproduced the *Arizona Networking News,* as well as organizing successful events in Phoenix.

"Often when we are alone together," Stan said, "I will speak Lee's thoughts as she thinks them."

A psychic acquaintance once told them that they had experienced many lifetimes together in very powerful positions.

"In this present life experience," Stan explains, "we would be of service to the many people who were our loyal followers in many previous life-times."

To this day, Stan Kalson and Lee Lagé continue to give each other personal love and support—and this translates into positive energy for spreading the concepts of holistic health to the widest possible audience.

Sixteen

Two Opposites Together

To the best of my recollection, I first met Lawrence Kennedy, Ph.D., in 1978. As a teacher of parapsychology who had undergone a number of dramatic metaphysical and E.T. (extraterrestrial) experiences, he had responded with great enthusiasm to my book *The Gods of Aquarius: UFOs and the Transformation of Man*. He arranged to meet me and we became friends and colleagues.

As Sherry has often remarked, one cannot help liking Lawrence, a robust, smiling, rugged man with contagious enthusiasm. He always has at least a dozen ideas scrambling around in his brain for immediate attention, and he tries to give as many of them equal time as he possibly can in any given hour of conversation.

Late in 1982, he came to my office with an attractive, well-spoken, well-educated young woman he introduced as his partner and business associate. I suspected the beginnings of a romantic involvement, despite the two seeming in nearly all ways to be complete opposites.

I liked Sandra Sitzmann immediately, but my inner voice kept whispering that their relationship would never last. But it is fourteen years later, and Lawrence and Sandra have truly found their destiny together.

"Our story is not one of love at first sight," Sandra admits. "It is, however, a tale of the 'gods at play,' and we often laugh about our love story being a grand cosmic joke."

I asked Sandra if she would help me tell their story of their destined love.

In the summer of 1981 in Omaha, Nebraska, Sandra Sitzmann, M.S., L.M.T., was busily packing and preparing for new and unknown adventures.

"I had just retired from the school system with fourteen years' experience as a professional teacher and guidance counselor. For the past seven years I had been feeling a growing restlessness to do something else with my life and my career."

But what? That was the nagging question. Why was she feeling this urgency to be somewhere else, doing something different?

She had no reason to be dissatisfied with her teaching career. She was well educated, proudly earning her master's degree by age twenty-seven. She had many good friends and a secure job guaranteeing a strong, steady income.

What else did she need?

Despite being well read and well traveled, Sandra had discovered she craved a deeper spiritual sense of herself and the universe. Humanistic, psychological, herbal, and health studies, extensive

reading, and a well-developed social consciousness
were not enough to quench the thirst of a searching soul that wanted to explore and experience life
without conventional restrictions.

"With supportive input from some friends and
the assistance of my astrologer friend Bob Mulligan, I began to break down the walls of fear I
had tenaciously clung to during my 'seven-year
itch.' I knew there was more to life than Nebraska's Big Red football team, apple pie, and the
American dream."

Mulligan encouraged her to eliminate her
worldly possessions—even to the extent of selling
her house. Sandra was proud of having bought a
house by herself at twenty-nine. When Bob told
her the house would sell by August 25, she began
packing, cleaning, and preparing to relocate and
adjust to a new life.

Mulligan had introduced her to the massage
technique called foot reflexology, and Sandra had
realized the deep, profound benefits of bodywork
combined with mental, emotional, and intuitive
levels of healing. Sandra applied and was accepted
as a student at the Boulder School of Massage
Therapy (also known as the Rocky Mountain
Healing Arts Institute). She had decided a career
in massage therapy would enable her to work
more effectively with the whole person.

Training started the first week in September,
and Sandra began to get a little nervous from the
time pressure. Was her house really going to sell
by August 25 and provide her with the money she
needed to move to Colorado and enroll in classes?

"Angels must have worked overtime to relieve

me of my worries," Sandra said, "because my house sold on the exact day Bob Mulligan said it would. As destiny would have it, a couple soon purchased my house so I could traipse off to Colorado. I made it to Boulder safe and sound for my first day of classes after driving all night. More angelic assistance!"

Simultaneous with the stresses, fears, and doubts of preparing for a major change in her life, Sandra underwent several unusual experiences that were synchronisitic to the story of how she met her destined love.

"I now have a better understanding as to the meaning and significance of these events. I remember participating in a heavenly initiation that was held specifically in my honor celebrating my rebirth and my decision to begin a new cycle in my life. It was so real—and I felt ecstatic and joyous! Evidently I passed my test of initiation and it was time to acknowledge that."

In August, Sandra's mother came to help her pack. Even with the assistance, Sandra felt overtired. She was emotionally sensitive to the fact that she was about to leave her home and friends.

"When I finally went to bed in the wee hours of the morning," Sandra said, "I heard computer-like sounds and saw multiple blinking lights—with my eyes open or closed! It all seemed so real in the physical sense, and it appeared to be occurring simultaneously inside my head and in another dimension, at another level of reality. I pinched my eyes tightly shut—and then played an 'open-and-closed game' for a while with the impressions persisting. After a while, the phantom images disappeared.

"Years later, after becoming involved with the
E.T. phenomenon and hearing how contact often
happens during emotionally trying times, I realized that this experience was preparing me for yet
another scenario in the next phase of my life."

During the late 1970s and early 1980s, Dr.
Lawrence Kennedy taught a series of classes entitled "I Can" in Lake Tahoe, California. The
theme was mind over matter, also known as psychokinesis. Lawrence says his life underwent a
360-degree turn after undergoing a near-death experience in 1971.

"Previously, I had undergone two near-death experiences, but this time I was clinically dead for
thirty minutes after two bleeding ulcers ruptured
simultaneously. Drastic changes occurred in my
life. My personality, beliefs, and values completely
reversed, and I left a lucrative job with a high-
paying salary as an advertising executive. I will-
ingly eliminated my material possessions and
terminated my marriage. The 'new' me returned
to postgraduate study, and after receiving a doc-
toral degree in parapsychology in 1973 and completing a course in mind control, I began to
research and teach about paranormal events, including spiritual psychic healing. I applied what I
had learned in the I Can classes."

Explaining his near-death experience, Lawrence
said:

I recall leaving my body and peering down
at it from the upper corner of the condo ceil-

ing. The physical me was doubled up into a
fetal position, hoping to alleviate the excru-
ciating pain. As I began to move through a
tunnel toward a bright light, I no longer felt
pain—nor did I have any feelings of concern
for my physical form—as images of my life
and emotions passed before my eyes. I continued to move toward the light and was ab-
sorbed in it. I was overwhelmed with
feelings of love and ecstasy. It was no longer
important that my physical body was non-
functioning as it lay on a blood-drenched
carpet. I basked in the brilliant light and felt
unattached to everything—except a nagging,
tugging force that seemed to be pulling me
back to the room where my body lay.

Lawrence said two radiant beings who called
themselves "Counselors" appeared to him in two
swirling cylinders of living light.

The frequency was almost more than I could
handle. Even though the two beings looked
like creatures from out of this world, the first
was so dazzlingly beautiful and radiated so
much love energy that I could barely stand
to look at her.

The female entity had white hair with almost violet highlights, lavender eyes, and appeared to be youthful, perhaps twenty-seven
years of age. She spoke telepathically in a
high girlish, sing-song voice and told me that
her name was Flameen, that she was from a
place called Venusia, and that we had known

DESTINED TO LOVE   165

each other in a past lifetime. I understood
that *Venusia* had nothing to do with the
planet Venus, but existed on another level of
reality. Her voice and words soothed me and
sounded like music in my head.

The other Counselor was male. At first his
appearance frightened me. He resembled a
kind of fish-man, and though he was decid-
edly 'different' looking, he was strangely
handsome. He wore a form-fitting silver
lamé suit that covered his muscular form. He
had large reptilian eyes and a slightly pointed
rise to his hairless forehead and scalp. I saw
scaley webbed hands, and he wore boots on
his feet.

In my head, I heard him say, 'If you cannot handle this appearance, I will change to
a form you can accept.' In a flash, he became another swirling cylinder of light. He
put me further at ease by changing his form
to one portraying the image of a handsome
Greek god, with a blond pageboy-style
hairdo and a short white tunic, trimmed in
electric blue.

The words that the two entities spoke to
Lawrence in unison astonished him. They said
Lawrence was about to lose his physical form be-
cause he had not completed what he had come to
Earth to do in his present life experience.

"I was shocked," Lawrence recalled. "I had
been programmed to believe I was a portrait of
success. After all, I had a great portfolio by the
age of thirty-three—comfort, recognition, female

companionship, an exciting nightlife, and all the 'toys' that money could buy."

The Counselors shocked him even further by pressing him to make a choice between staying and completing what he came to do—or leaving.

As a single father, Lawrence was concerned about leaving his young son. Who would take care of him? Was he ready to leave his family and friends to face the unknown?

"And then," Lawrence said, "the universe silently spoke to me, enlightening me with profound truths, instilling within me an incredible knowledge and an awesome sense of the God-force."

Lawrence remembered how at the age of seven, he had boldly proclaimed himself never to be spiritually controlled by the dogmatic rules of the church which had denied his mother communion after she had become a divorcee. He had argued that no loving God would allow such an injustice, questioned the authority of the church, and vowed never again to return to that particular church's rigid beliefs and regulations.

But now he was embracing and comprehending God beyond what mere words could ever describe.

"I made my decision," Lawrence said. "I knew that I must return and begin the real work of my life. I could not precisely define it, but I knew it was to deliver truth and love to others.

"The Counselors knew my every thought and telepathically responded: 'We are here to assist you on your return to the body. After a while, others will follow us to continue helping you progress into your new states of consciousness.'"

Lawrence quickly and repeatedly received the

assistance that the other-worldly entities had promised.

"My medical doctor examined my 'after-death' x-rays and was amazed to find my bleeding ulcers completely gone, with no scars remaining! After this experience, I became a believer. Of *what*, I did not yet fully comprehend!"

Inspired by Spirit, Lawrence became driven to speak on free will and choice, teaching about the existence of life at other levels and universes. He taught the I Can classes, graduating nine hundred eager participants over a seven-year period. In 1980, he was mysteriously funded to participate in an expedition to Egypt to research the ancient Egyptian-Pleiadian connection, to prove their existence, and review their history.

After meeting with retired colonel Wendelle Stevens, a UFO investigator, and becoming involved in the Billy Meiers-Pleiadian connection, he moved to Sedona, Arizona. The Meiers case had left an indelible imprint on Lawrence, and he began to work on the *Pleiadian Connection* film series that later became a part of the *Cosmic Connection* video.

In 1982, Lawrence Kennedy was in Colorado, making a guest appearance at Dael Walker's crystallography class. Walker had invited Lawrence to take some Kirlian aura photos of participating members to show how the crystal healing work affected their bioelectric energy. Sandra Sitzmann was a member of the class, but neither took much notice of the other.

"Later, at a party, I was demonstrating spoon bending through PK (psychokinesis) to an interested audience that had crowded into a small room," Lawrence recalled. "Sandra entered the room and sat next to me on the couch. I do not recall accidentally sloshing wine on her, but she insists that this was her second brief introduction to me—and she was not too impressed with it. However, Spirit continued to play cupid."

Sandra remembered that Lawrence's assistant, Lenore Cullin, kept encouraging her to try Dr. Kennedy's special eye treatment program because he had been achieving some remarkable results.

"I was involved in another holistic eye program with a local doctor, and I was excited to find someone who might be able to assist me with new methods," Sandra said. "It was an extraordinary experience, and my eyes showed signs of improvement after only one session."

She was so impressed that she arranged for Dr. Kennedy to take Kirlian photographs at a group meeting of Reiki healers that she had organized in Boulder.

"He very effectively demonstrated the affects before and after a healing session," Sandra said. "But afterward, he began to converse about extraterrestrial intelligence. I was now sure this man was far out, and I had no intention of getting mixed up with a space cadet!"

At the same time, Sandra couldn't deny she was intrigued by Dr. Kennedy's knowledge and understanding of things she had never heard about before. Seemingly out of nowhere, he asked her to assist him in putting together an E.T. ball in Boulder on Halloween eve of 1982.

"Why me?" Sandra exclaimed. Her reluctance

turned to enthusiasm and the E.T. Ball was an event to remember.

They managed to pull it off with two bands playing and a radio disc jockey announcing and awarding prizes to the best-costumed "extraterrestrials" at the "Come as You Were" Ball. They still talk about this fun-filled event as a significant catalyst to the beginning of their relationship.

After successfully accomplishing the showy event, Lawrence suggested that they travel to Arizona and meet with me, retired Colonel Wendelle Stevens and Jim Diletoso, a computer analyst who was expert at detecting the authenticity of UFO evidence.

"Why not?" Sandra thought. "I had just graduated from massage school. I could work in Phoenix as well as anywhere else. It was as good a time as any to pursue the dream. Lawrence and I were then more involved as partners in business than in a romantic relationship."

Many seasons have come and gone as Sandra and Lawrence have traveled throughout the Southwest and Northwest. The threads of their encounters primarily weave together the Pleiadian-cosmic-universal theme and the interrelated themes of health, electrophotography, earth changes, and the environment.

The two have bonded on many multidimensional levels and have created Starline Unlimited, a service-product-oriented company; High Quest, a community-focused project; Link-Up/Up-Link, a networking vehicle; the *Cosmic Connection,* a videotape with a right-brain approach to the E.T.-Star People connection; and the Hiva, a sustainable prefab structure using natural, recycled materials for shelters, greenhouses, and therapeutic centers.

How do apparently extreme opposites such as Lawrence Kennedy and Sandra Sitzmann manage to stay together and accomplish so many high-energy projects?

Sandra suggests that a partial answer may be that wholeness can be achieved when opposite qualities exist in harmony and balance through nonjudgment, acceptance, and lack of fear.

"He speaks and I write. He is objective and I am subjective. He dreams about the architectural drawings, and I attend to the details as we build foundations together. It takes two sides of a coin to create the whole, the balance, the unity.

"We continue to transmute addictions, ego issues, and power struggles within a relationship between two strong-willed and independent individuals. Transmuting the dross of the base metal (ego) by fire through endurance, patience, courage, and commitment to a greater universal cause has polished our stars to a brighter sheen of gold. When our halos get tarnished, more polishing with tolerance and more buffing with tender loving care is required. Just as fine, minute particles of sand constantly irritate the shell of the oyster to produce a beautiful pearl, so, too, are our annoying, repetitive, and addictive habits eventually transmuted to the wonderful gifts of acceptance, unconditional love, joy, and consciousness.

"We do not pretend that our relationship is easy

or even perfected yet. Life continues in a never-ending and ever-expanding circle and spiral on the humanistic and dualistic merry-go-round.

"Our ties to each other have universal origins, and the assistance and support of a greater energy force from beyond the stars is recognized.

"Our journey continues with a spiritual commitment to a Higher Power and each other, knowing that we are evolving as greater galactic beings in the sea of energy for our own benefit and for the good of all."

Seventeen

Destiny Reunites Twin Flames

Patrick Flanagan and Gael Crystal Flanagan regard the story of how they got together as a modern-day fairy tale. In their opinion, there is no question that destiny played an important role in reuniting "twin flames."

I first met Patrick in Honolulu in February of 1972. At that time, he encouraged me to join him inside a large plastic pyramid he had built as a portable meditation device.

Since that time, he has greatly enlarged his research program on pyramidal energies, written numerous books on the subject, marketed a wide variety of items, and established workshops on the transformation of various body energy fields into higher consciousness. As one of the "fathers" of longevity research, Patrick believes that we can eliminate practically all disease, purify our polluted air and water, and prolong human life for decades by applications of various scientific health modalities he has developed over many years.

People are more inclined to believe Patrick Flanagan when he makes extraordinary claims because he has been harvesting the groves of science since he was eleven years old. When he was seventeen, he gained international recognition for his invention of the Neurophone, an electronic hearing aid that allows deaf people to hear by bypassing the ears and transmitting sounds directly to the brain. Before he was out of his teens, *Life* magazine had listed Patrick as one of the top scientists in the nation.

In July 1982, ten years after I had met Patrick, I met his destined love, Gael Crystal, a nationally known writer and health and longevity researcher, when I was filming a seminar at the Camelback Inn in Scottsdale, Arizona, for inclusion in a video on past life research that I was producing.

"I had been living on the island of Eleuthera in the Bahamas," Gael said. "One night I had a very vivid dream in which I saw myself in a beautiful room full of many bright and unusual objects that looked like crystals of all shapes and sizes. I was sitting across from a little brown-haired man with a beard who seemed to be predicting my future. Just before the dream ended, he levitated the table between us. When I woke up, I tried to remember what was being said, but all I could recall was that he was predicting some important event in my future."

About two years later, after she'd packed for a trip to Australia and the Orient, Gael received a brochure advertising a seminar in Scottsdale. Among the featured key speakers would be scientist Patrick Flanagan, inventor and "Father of Pyramid Power."

Although she rarely attended seminars, Gael said that she was drawn to this particular gathering by an inner prompting from Spirit that was quite strong. Without further deliberation, she decided to postpone her world travel plans and head for Scottsdale.

The first time she and Patrick came into physical contact in their present life experience was on stage in front of hundreds of people as he selected her from the audience to demonstrate the secret Hopi handshake.

Later Patrick told her, "I thought you were a most beautiful soul, and I felt that somehow I had always known you. I knew that we would meet again."

Both knew that they had felt a special connection on a Higher-Self plane, and the resonance of their initial meeting continued even after they had returned to their homes. Patrick was living in Brentwood, on the western edge of Los Angeles, and Gael had decided to move to the middle of the Angeles National Forest to live in a house full of quartz crystals and semi-precious stones.

"The forest offered me a quiet environment of tall pine trees and a creek that ran through the property a few feet from my door," Gael said. "I spent my days in meditation, writing, and research."

On a day that Gael comfortably terms "fateful," she received a telephone call from a friend who wanted to tell her of an amazingly accurate reading that she had just received from a very special psychic-sensitive.

As they spoke, Gael felt a tremendous sensation

of *déjà vu,* and she vividly recalled the dream
she'd had two years before, in the Bahamas, about
the brown-haired, bearded man who levitated a table and made a prediction.

"I realized that something important was about
to happen in my life," she said. "Tell me," she
asked her friend, "Does this amazing psychic of
yours have brown hair and a beard?"

"Why, yes, he does."

"And does he also levitate tables?"

Once again, she received an affirmative answer.

"But how do you know . . . ?" the woman
asked.

Gael told her friend about her dream, and she
asked her to bring the psychic-sensitive to her
house as soon as it could be arranged.

"When the psychic arrived, I immediately recognized him from my dream," Gael said. "He responded to the energy of my house full of
crystals, and he remarked, 'I don't know if it is
you or all these crystals, but I've never experienced so much energy in my life!' "

During the course of the reading he did for
Gael, he asked her, "Who is Pat?"

Gael paused, then remembered her meeting with
Patrick Flanagan a few months earlier.

"Yes, that's him," the psychic affirmed. "You
will meet again soon, and you will cross the ocean
together. You will help him to discover something
that will greatly benefit humankind. It has something to do with water and rejuvenation. You will
do great things together as you have done in past
lifetimes, and you will be together for the rest of
your lives."

Gael's head was spinning as the psychic spoke on, making seemingly outrageous predictions.

"I am getting strong impressions of the importance of the discoveries you'll both make together," the psychic continued. "They'll help a great many people all over the world."

Gael asked when these things would occur.

"Soon. Very soon," he said.

Before he left, Gael told him about the dream in which she had watched him levitating a table.

"From time to time, if the energy is right, I can use combined energies to lift a table an inch or two off the floor," he said, then demonstrated his remarkable ability.

Less than three months later, Gael was invited to be a keynote speaker at a seminar in Scottsdale. Patrick Flanagan was invited to speak at the same seminar.

Earlier that year, Patrick had been contacted by a well-known psychic-astrologer who told him that he would meet his lifemate at a seminar where he would be speaking. His destined mate would have long, dark hair with reddish highlights. She would be a Taurus and would have come originally from northeastern United States.

At the time, Patrick was conducting seminars all over the country on a variety of subjects, so he knew that it was not out of the question for him to connect with his preordained mate at such a gathering.

In July 1983, Patrick entered a large room at the seminar in Scottsdale where hundreds of people were milling around between lectures. The moment he spotted Gael standing near the seminar registration desk, he walked straight up to her.

"Are you a Taurus by any chance?" he asked.

Gael smiled at the direct question. "Yes."

"Are you originally from the Northeast?" Patrick pushed onward with his spontaneous interrogation.

"Yes," she said. "Do I win some kind of prize for answering both questions correctly?"

Patrick laughed and took her hand. "Yes, you win me!"

While Gael studied him for some clue, he quickly explained: "It sounds incredible, but a psychic-astrologer told me that I would meet my lifemate at a seminar and that she would be a Taurus from the Northeast who had long, dark hair with reddish highlights. You match the description perfectly! I just knew it was you the moment I saw you."

Patrick's facial expressions seemed to be begging her to understand that he was not some raving lunatic, and Gael felt an instant connection. She was already beginning the process of recognition that Patrick Flanagan truly was her twin flame.

"What else did this astrologer tell you?" Gael asked.

Encouraged by her willingness to hear him out, Patrick continued, "She said that you would give me the love, support, and commitment that no one else could provide."

"Really?" Gael said, feeling a surge of love toward him.

"She also said we'd marry, move to the mountains, and be happy for the rest of our lives."

Soon after the seminar was over, Patrick invited Gael to join him for a weekend. "It was a weekend from which neither of us returned to our former life," Gael commented.

Once, while meditating together, they experienced a simultaneously received past-life memory. In a prior life experience, they were Alessandro and Seraphina Cagliostro, eighteenth-century metaphysicians, healers, and alchemists. The Cagliostros were very close to the Count St. Germain, and they were initiated by him into the order of the Knights Templar. Seraphina enjoyed the honor of being the first woman initiated into the order.

"Like the Cagliostros, we also work together formulating rejuvenating elixirs and sharing teachings on the development of the higher spiritual self," Gael said.

The Flanagans have had their previous lifetime together as Alessandro and Seraphina confirmed by several well-known psychic-sensitives, including Lazaris.

When Patrick and Gael decided to get married, they travelled to Egypt to be joined as one in the Great Pyramid of Giza during the Pleiadian alignment of 1983.

"This auspicious astrological alignment happens only once every 4,800 years," Gael said. "It occurs when the full moon is directly over the top of the pyramid, in direct alignment with the Pleiades."

In Egypt, destiny once more played its part in

their lives. There was no precedent for the Egyptian officials to grant permission for them to get married in the Great Pyramid, as it had never been done before.

"Permission was granted," Gael said, "and we spent three intense days and nights meditating and celebrating in the king's and queen's chambers with a small circle of friends. On the third night of the Pleiadian alignment, with the full moon shining directly over the top of the Great Pyramid, we climbed to the top and spent the entire night in meditation."

After visiting the sacred temples of Egypt and Greece, the Flanagans returned to their secluded home near Sedona, Arizona, and began a fast.

On the twenty-second day of their fast, Patrick and Gael began speaking about the spiritual, as well as the physiological, importance of water. They discussed how, throughout history, sacred temples and sites had usually been built on special energy locations where water played a significant role in the generation of certain specific and powerful energies.

Patrick told Gael about his lifelong quest to duplicate the special energy properties of Hunza water. (Hunza is a remote valley in Pakistan enclosed by Himalayan mountain peaks. The residents there are said to possess certain health secrets which enable some of them to live in excess of 150 years.) He told her how his friend and mentor, Dr. Henri Coanda, had started him on the quest over twenty years before.

"That night," Gael said, "we went into our laboratory and created our Crystal Energy™ concentrate. Through a special thirty-three-step process, we created a laboratory analog of the water that is found in the Hunza Valley.

"We went six months living on juices and smoothies, putting our Crystal Energy™ into all our beverages. During this period we were exercising, writing, creating, and feeling better than ever."

Impressed by the Flanagans' bright eyes and robust health, their friends began to request the "elixir," and soon Patrick and Gael began producing it in ever increasing quantities. It is now used by tens of thousands of people all over the world. They have even written a book on the concentrate entitled *Elixir of the Ageless*.

Like the alchemists of old, Patrick and Gael spend almost all their time creating life-enhancing and health-giving formulations in their laboratory-home, venturing out into the world on rare occasions. They work with the latest high-tech equipment—some of which they have specially designed for their pioneering research into longevity and bioenergy systems.

The Flanagans live a quietly active lifestyle on a remote, twenty-odd acre "hermitage," surrounded by wildlife. Although my wife, Sherry, and I have known them for decades, we have not seen them for many years, keeping in touch mainly by telephone and fax. We respect their need for seclusion, and we know their pets keep them from being lonely.

As a mutual friend and reincarnationist has commented, "Patrick and Gael Flanagan are a perfect example of soulmates with shared dharma in the areas of science and service."

Dharma is defined as your duty to yourself and to society. Some see it as their true purpose in life.

As longtime spiritual beings, the twin-flames of Patrick and Gael Flanagan have embarked once again on a journey of discovery on all levels. They have now been married for over twelve years, and their love and their life together continue to flourish.

Eighteen

She Found Her Knight

One of the marvelous benefits of being an author is the opportunity to meet many colorful people. In some instances, such a meeting develops into a friendship spanning many years. In 1983, I was introduced to John Hobson by a mutual friend and we have remained constant allies and confidants ever since.

Although the public may know John as the tough, two-fisted former cop who headed his own "A-Team," a select handful of men who flew to foreign countries to rescue U.S. citizens held captive by terrorists, I know him as an excellent artist and woodcarver.

While government officials recognize him as the specialist responsible for having established the security systems of many nuclear plants, I recognize him as a sensitive man who unashamedly allows his tears to flow.

While dozens of Hollywood celebrities regard him as their highly capable personal bodyguard, I regard him as a friend who blushes if I compli-

ment him and gets goosebumps if I share a
spooky story.

In addition to all of the above, I know John as
an individual who came to rely on all six of his
senses and his guardian angel to get him out of
tight spots. Not long ago, John and I met with
representatives of a major Hollywood studio who
have expressed interest in dramatizing some of our
adventures in a television series.

Although John was on the periphery of the
movieland scene for years, working sometimes as
a technical adviser, other times as a bodyguard,
and on occasion, as an actor, about nine years ago,
the cinema bug bit him hard.

"I've lived the kinds of roles Sly Stallone and
Chuck Norris play," John would grouse. "My
true-life adventures beat anything that I see in the
movies or on television. I feel I've got to go to
Hollywood to give it a try."

"Go for it," I encouraged him. "You're no kid
anymore, but you've still got a good physique and
more ambition than any ten thirty-year-olds. Besides, you're a damn good storyteller. You can
write your own scripts and act in them."

In 1992, when I was in Los Angeles to give a
speech, I got a call from John.

"I'm coming to your lecture," he said.

I told him I would leave a pass for him at the
registration desk.

"I'm bringing my attorney with me," he added.

No problem, I assured him. I would leave two
passes.

When I met the lovely young woman John introduced as his attorney, my inner guidance tickled

my solar plexus, and I picked up that Lisa the lawyer was most definitely a "keeper." As someone who wished only the very best for John, I prayed that he knew it.

Thanks to the angels of love, on August 18, 1995, John and Lisa were married, and they left on a European honeymoon.

But before they went, I got their separate stories on how they felt the sure hand of destiny brought them together.

"I guess I was always too busy getting my life together to allow time for a serious relationship," Lisa said. "My mother, Loretta, was always trying to get me interested in the guys who visited our home. Although they were usually friends of mine, I would always end up finding fault with them.

"My friends and family would comment that I was too picky. I usually did not go out with a fellow for more than one or two dates, because I knew I just wasn't interested. In my opinion, I was just being a smart girl. I was determined to do something with my life before I settled down and had a family."

During law school, Lisa began to feel an overwhelming loneliness, as if a void in her life needed to be filled. "After I broke up with a young man who had chased me from high school to college to law school, I felt I was never going to find someone just right for me. On the other hand, I was glad I hadn't gotten married earlier, because I'd changed my expectations of what a relationship should be. I'm certain an earlier marriage would only have ended in divorce or an outside affair."

Lisa decided to develop her spiritual side. "I began to meditate. I attended New Age courses, began to interpret signs, and kept a journal of my dreams. I prayed to God that I would find a husband with whom I could spend the rest of my life. I even bought a stone in the shape of a frog and stroked it while meditating to attract true love."

Sensing Lisa's frustrations, her mother asked her if she wanted to meet an actor friend who hung out with her crowd.

"Oh, great," Lisa sighed, unfairly equating "actor" with "flake."

Loretta tried to tell her that this man was far more than just an actor.

Lisa was beginning to become a bit more interested, but when her mother indicated that he was an older man, Lisa nixed the meeting.

But Loretta was persistent, and eventually, Lisa met John Hobson.

"Although John is an attractive man with a strong physique," Lisa acknowledged, "there were no sparks flying."

Then, through one of those little twists of fate, John came to live temporarily at Loretta's place.

"I would have long talks with him when I came to visit," Lisa said. "Soon we would just hang out together, and we became good friends. We went to museums, movies, and lunch. I began to notice that it was nice to be close to him."

One evening her mother asked John to tell Lisa some stories about his "other life."

"That night, I heard about so many courageous adventures that he had undergone that my head was spinning," Lisa recalled. "I couldn't put John

in any mold. It seemed he'd always pursued truth
and justice from many different careers.

"That same evening he gave me a collection of
the articles written about him. I was impressed.
When I read the article by Brad Steiger that referred to John as a modern Knight Errant, tears
welled up in my eyes, and I asked myself if he
could be the knight for whom I had searched all
my life."

It was soon after that fateful evening that John
asked her to represent him in his career as actor
and screenwriter.

"I took this as an invitation to get more involved with him. We met for lunch to discuss our
plans. Soon after, we began dating—nine months
after we had met."

Their first trip together was a ski weekend in
Arizona. "We talked all the way on the drive," Lisa
said. "It was then that John confided in me that he
had learned through a past-life regression that he
had a spirit guide in the form of a wolf that had
followed him through time from a life where he
and the woman he loved had been killed by angry
villagers. The wolf had promised always to be his
protector.

"When he told me this, John had goosebumps.
There were tears in his eyes. Because he had confided in me, I was deeply touched, and I felt very
close to him—which was a good thing, because
when we got to the hotel, there was only one bed
in the room!

"The first time I told John I loved him, he was
dumbfounded. I said it a number of times that
evening. Later, he told me that each time he had

mentally asked his spirit guide what I was thinking, I had told him that I loved him.

"Soon after this trip, we moved in together. One day I hugged John and blurted, 'Would you marry me?' It kind of fell off my tongue before I even thought about it. He said yes."

John Hobson had always been a responsible father to his two sons. Although he had traveled the globe rescuing U.S. citizens kidnapped in foreign countries, he was always home on the holidays and special days.

"But I had been divorced for many years," he recalled, "and there was always something missing. I don't believe man was made to live alone. I wanted so much to have that certain woman in my life—but she just wasn't there. Don't get me wrong—I had plenty of opportunities—but nobody had come into my life that I wanted to spend forever with."

John painfully remembers many a Christmas Eve wrapping gifts for his children and his parents with tearing eyes, feeling empty in his heart, "Not for lack of love from my family, but for someone other than family to love."

Superficially, John tried to project the macho image others held of him, but he admitted that he steadily prayed for that special woman to come into his lonely life.

Nor could he ever talk to his fellow operatives about something so heavenly as his guardian angel. "She had the brightest blond hair. I was never able to see her features. In time of danger, she would often appear as one of God's creatures. I

knew that she was real, and she proved her powers
to me many times."

About the same time that John got the movie
bug and Hollywood began expressing interest in
his unique talents and the incredible stories that
he had to tell, his boys were reaching their "own
life" age, somewhere, he joked, between "knowing
wrong and doing wrong."

"My oldest son was getting married, and my
youngest was in his second year of college," he
said, "so I left a million-dollar home, a new Por-
sche, my family, and, it seemed, everything I had
worked for, and moved to Tinseltown to become a
movie star."

John's new home in California was a storage
room above his cousin's roller-skating rink.

"No windows, no toilet, and the pigeons flew
in and out of the broken-down building," John
recalled with a grimace. "Every weekend, the
various teen gangs would patronize the rink, and
there was always the threat of a shootout. I would
sit alone in my storage-room home and wonder if
I was an idiot for trying to become a movie star
at my age—an idol for the aged."

During the first six months of his new life, John
tried to go back to Phoenix and his old life as
often as possible. Sometimes on those long drives,
he would think about predictions that psychic Jan
Ross had made in 1985.

"She told me I was going to become involved
in the movie business and write about my exploits.
I would move to California, meet a blonde-blonde
woman, get married, and have two children. I
would not stay in California because of the nega-

tive atmosphere, and I would probably move to the East Coast to live out my life. But now, here I was, six years later, living in a skid row apartment and broke, even though Orion had optioned a screenplay and I had costarred in a movie."

John had just decided to desert Tinseltown and head back for Phoenix for good when his friend Loretta invited him to move into her guestroom. He wouldn't have to pay rent; he could get out of his pigeon-infested dump; and he could still pursue his movie career.

It was on an outing with Loretta, her daughter, Gina, and her boyfriend, Rick, that John met Loretta's older daughter, an attorney named Lisa.

"Lisa sat next me," John remembered, "but I felt that neither of us had any interest in the other. The music was loud. At one point I forgot myself and made a comment about attorneys being like sharks. That didn't help to cement our relationship."

The night ended so uneventfully that a few weeks later, John talked a recently divorced friend of his into asking Lisa out. No sparks there, either. Both later reported to John that the other had a "nice personality."

John still travelled to Phoenix every other weekend. "It was during these long hours on the empty road that I would speak to God and my guardian angel. Though I'm Irish Catholic, religion was never a part of my upbringing.

"But through my own pain and turmoil, I had developed my own relationship with the Supreme Power. On more than one occasion, my guardian angel came to me, dodging bullets and kept me alive. I had spent many hours speaking to this angel, asking her for help. I truly wanted a love relationship in my life. It wasn't happening, but I didn't give up."

During the next several months, Lisa would visit her mother's house regularly. As a group, they would go to the beach or to dinner.

"It felt so relaxed to be with Lisa," John said. "She was so genuine in her heart. I had never met anyone who could laugh at herself like Lisa could. She didn't get angry. She enjoyed herself. I was learning something of life."

John can't quite put his finger on the point when Lisa changed. Or maybe he changed. Or maybe there was no change at all.

"But we were spending more and more time together. And it was all very different for me. Lisa was becoming my best friend. I was feeling something for my friend Lisa that I had never felt before.

"Then I'd become frightened, fearing that I was reading something into our relationship that wasn't mutual. Did she really care for me the way I cared for her? Oh, dear guardian angel, please help me!"

John recalled very clearly the Tuesday night when Lisa was leaving on an overnight in Riverside for a trial. He was heading again for Phoenix. They had agreed to meet for dinner before she left that night.

While they were saying goodbye, John asked himself if he was prepared to be humiliated. "I leaned into Lisa's car and kissed her. Rain made the parking lot very wet, and while I was making myself vulnerable, my feet were sliding on the pavement and I was shrinking, getting shorter and shorter. Lisa didn't notice. But more important, she kissed me back."

From that point on, John said, they became even closer friends, and he began to share things with Lisa that he had never before shared with anyone—powerful, spiritual events that had taken place in his life. He was experiencing something that he had never before felt in a relationship—absolute trust.

Lisa said that on Thanksgiving Day 1994, she and John were in Wilmington, North Carolina. "For some reason I had worn a ring made of crystal baguettes to dinner. While we waited in the bar for our table, I joked with John about marrying me. Didn't he remember giving me this crystal engagement ring?

"After we moved to our table, I asked him again if he was going to marry me, and he said, 'Well, where's *my* ring?' I gave him the crystal ring I was wearing. He then asked me if I would marry him and said, 'Here's *your* ring.' Out came a case with my engagement ring! He had switched the rings like a magician!

"Thank you, Mom! Thank you, Wolf! Thank you, Angel!"

Nineteen

Angelic Beings Saved Him
for His Soulmate

David Jungclaus told me that he and his wife, Barbara, are firm believers that the Mother-Father God's love blesses us mortals with angelic beings, soul mates, spiritual guides, teachers, and spirit helpers.

David, author of *The City Beneath the Bermuda Triangle,* says he and Barbara freely acknowledge that Divine Guidance from the Cosmos has played an instrumental part in their lives—on both aware and subconscious levels.

"Angelic Beings not only brought us together as man and wife, but we have both been guided by such entities throughout our lives.

"The most interesting part of such spiritual guidance, is that you don't have to be a religious person or have any real understanding of the spiritual process involved. Such guidance is part of the Divine Plan to help all souls. Once you *do* become aware of the work of angelic entities, you realize that it is one of the greatest gifts you can receive."

David admitted that although Barbara and he are acutely aware of the guidance of angelic beings today, it was not always so.

"Neither of us knew until much later in our lives that angelic entities were helping to chart our spiritual destiny—both apart and together."

David believes we choose our parents and our birth environments for many different reasons— from wishing to return to be with those who form our spiritual family, to working out painful karmic lessons.

He knows very little about his parents because they were killed in a car accident when he was only a year old.

"I had the misfortune of being placed in a San Francisco orphanage at the time of the 1929 Depression, and such institutions were filled to overflowing and very underfinanced.

"But angelic guidance was already at work to compensate. Two wealthy volunteers at the orphanage told a couple they knew about the new baby."

The Jungclauses were warned of the baby's ill health. "Thankfully, it posed no problems to my new parents, for they were Christian Scientists and my mother was a healer. An act of true angelic guidance manifested at a time of financial crises. My father became a first reader at the First Christian Science Church in San Francisco and received a large salary."

David remembers that at the age of five he had a regular nocturnal visitor.

"I had my own bedroom, which faced the backyard, the fence, and the forest behind it. In the evenings, I would often see a dwarf sitting on the fence. In recent years, I have spoken to many UFO contactees who have shared similar experiences with dwarfs, fairies, and other magical beings. I believe that they are the guardians that monitor, communicate, guide, and protect us."

When David was nine, the invisible force of angelic protection saved him from being murdered by a man who preyed upon children.

"Even today, when I remember the incident, I can feel the chill wind of death's wings.

"Parents can only warn their children and establish rules to help them and protect them. Sooner or later, however, the child is probably going to break some of those rules. One rule that I broke often was to thumb a ride home from school."

David recalls that it was late one afternoon when he thumbed a ride home from downtown San Francisco.

"An inner alarm of fear sounded as I got into the paneled meat delivery truck and discovered that there were no door handles. A cold chill made me shudder. The truck was not air conditioned, and it had a foul smell to it. The driver was behaving in a weird manner. His clothes were dirty, just like the inside of the truck."

David was frightened by the man's eyes, which leered at him through thick lenses. The man began talking dirty, and he was nearly paralyzed with fear when he noticed for the first time a coil of rope and a roll of tape at his feet.

But a soft angelic voice told David to remain

calm. "Try to act natural," the voice said. "If you make him uneasy, he will hurt you. Stay very calm."

David said it was as if the angelic being was sitting directly behind him.

"Face the man and talk to him. Don't let him know that you're afraid of him. Take your hand and slowly move it behind you—and roll down the window."

Somehow, David managed to get the window rolled down without the driver noticing.

"He was starting to get very excited as we neared an uninhabited mountain area. The angelic being said, 'Be alert and don't show fear.' The soothing voice calmed me as I fought the panic inside me. My heart was beating so loud I was certain the driver could hear it."

David did his best to fight fear as the driver started rubbing his crotch and slowed the truck to a near stop. A sick smile stretched the man's lips, and sweat moistened the grime on his face.

"Be ready!" the angelic being warned.

The driver slowly unzipped his fly. "He started laughing, then asked, 'Do you want to see my forty-five?'

"My angel guide told me to make my move. I don't know how I jumped out the window, but I did. The last glance I had of the driver was of his pulling a .45 automatic out of his pants.

"I ran and ran until I reached people. I didn't tell anyone what had happened—especially my parents, as I knew I'd be in big trouble for having thumbed a ride. The angelic voice had saved me from a killer!"

At a Halloween party in college, David met the girl of his dreams.

"She was just gorgeous. Her blue eyes drew me like a moth to a flame. It was instant love. It was as if two magnets had been pulled together. From that moment on, I couldn't eat, dream, or sleep without longing for her."

Barbara was a senior in high school, and the two of them soon began dating and spending all their free time together. Weekdays they would do their homework at her house.

"We were soon going steady, but neither of us was seriously thinking of marriage. We both said we weren't ready to settle down. Barbara didn't want to get married until after she had done a lot of traveling.

"All the traveling she got, however, was a honeymoon trip to Palm Springs!"

David and Barbara let their love grow and soon were planning for parenthood.

"Angelic guidance found us a home out of the city, and our life was very happy. We have brought into the world five wonderful children—four girls and a boy."

David remembered one morning rather early in their marriage when Barbara lay in bed, looking out the window and watching a family of birds in a large oak tree.

"Suddenly, she exclaimed, 'There's a dwarf sitting in the tree looking at us!'

"I turned just in time to get a quick look," David said. "It was *him,* my dwarf friend from childhood. I had a total recall of my earlier experiences, and I told Barbara all about him."

Twenty

She Could Not Resist
Her Destined Love

In January 1987, thirty-six-year-old Laura Wesson found herself dumped in Barbados without a clue as to what she would do next.

"I had been in show business since I was eleven," she said, "and on my own since I was eighteen. I had been an entertainer on cruise ships for ten years, and my goal was to become a cruise director. I was literally the darling of this particular ship—until a new assistant cruise director came on board. For some reason, he didn't like me. I tried to rise above his negativity, but he kept at management until he got me fired."

As a practicing Christian Scientist for over twenty years, Laura had the spiritual stamina to resist falling apart emotionally over such unfair treatment.

"I somehow felt that everything would be all right," she recalled. "I had an inner knowing that I was being directed elsewhere. I just had no idea at the time where that would be."

From the age of eighteen until her late twenties, Laura had been gifted with psychic ability.

"My angels were with me whenever I most needed them during those years," she said. "I often heard a male voice directing me and providing me with accurate predictions. When I needed the most help, I would receive messages through jewelry pieces that I found in the streets.

"Perhaps the most outrageous example of this unusual angelic process is the time when I was in New York, sitting in a rented car, feeling very depressed. I was actually thinking of ending it all when my hand fell to the spot where the back seat meets the bottom cushion and my finger touched something metallic. When I grabbed the object and held it up in front of my face, I saw that it was a piece of jewelry that had four letters hanging horizontally, reading 'L . . . I . . . V . . . E.' The funny thing is, all those life-saving jewelry pieces that I had collected over the years have simply disappeared."

At the age of twenty-three, Laura planned to marry a man she believed to be her soulmate.

"Robert was also twenty-three, separated, with two small children. When I told the good news to an acquaintance of mine, an accomplished palmist, her response was, 'Oh, no, dear, I don't think so. You won't marry until you're thirty-six. And when you do, it will be to a man who'll change your life forever.'

"Sadly, Robert became deathly ill due to internal conflict from his love for me and his responsibility to his young family."

One evening, as he lay in his bed gasping for

air and Laura sat prayerfully in the living room, she heard a male voice say loudly in her head, "Robert must go back to his wife, Holly!"

Robert stood in the doorway, perfectly healed and almost glowing, and said quietly, "I must tell you something. I heard a male voice . . . that . . . told me that I must return to Holly. And then I was instantly healed."

The moment she'd seen him in the doorway, Laura had known what he was going to say. She said she'd been told the same thing, then they both began to cry.

It took Laura two years to get over her loss. Her palmist friend had been correct. But she had also promised Laura a man that would change her life forever.

"I had to wait thirteen years!" Laura said. "But I used to 'talk' to him all the time. I would climb to the upper decks of the ships on which I entertained and yell at the stars, 'Where the hell are you? Why do I have to wait so long?' "

What Laura did not know during those lonely nights aboard ship is that sometime during those thirteen years a successful Houston businessman named Dan Clausing was standing at the bay window of his office penthouse, suddenly realizing that even with all his wealth, he was very unhappy. At that moment of awareness, he heard a male voice in the room say very clearly, *"Either get on with what you came here to do—or check out!"*

As a rational businessman, he had difficulty accepting an unsolicited ultimatum from an unseen source, but the voice came again: *"Either get on with what you came here to do—or leave the ve-hicle!"*

Dan sat down at his desk in bewilderment—and resolved to ignore this unknown, unseen intruder.

Three weeks later, when he came down with a life-threatening illness, he recalled the warning voice.

Three months later, he gave up everything that he thought he had held dear—his failed marriage, his estate, his wealth, his businesses—and set out to make an avocation in metaphysics his new vocation. He worked with Bob Monroe for three years, and took his program on the road.

In January 1987 Laura was left in Barbados by the cruise ship on which she had been so happily employed, with her luggage and little else. She remained calm and assured that wonderful new opportunities were waiting for her right around some marvelous cosmic corner.

Laura's mother had always been her number-one supporter, so she eventually went to her mother's home in Los Altos, California. Soon after her arrival, Laura decided to drive to Santa Cruz to attend a seminar at a Roman Catholic retreat sponsored by the Monroe Institute.

"Mother was intensely adamant that I *not* attend the Gateway Voyager seminar in Santa Cruz," Laura recalled. "She even threatened to disown me if I attended. She carried on about the event being occult, New Age, satanic, and everything else, and she was afraid that I would end up brain-washed and in a cult."

At last, with Laura's promise to leave immediately if there were any satanic shenanigans, her mother relented, and Laura made plans to drive the forty miles to Santa Cruz. The seminar brochure indicated that the facilitator of the event was Dan Clausing—a name that meant nothing to Laura.

Neither did the name mean anything to a talented psychic-sensitive named Mary, who kept hearing the name in meditation one evening. A male voice had intruded in her reverie and told her to "call Dan Clausing."

After the command had repeated itself, Mary decided to call her friend Vicki, another talented psychic, to see if she might have any insight into the matter.

"Yes," Vicki surprised her. "I know Dan Clausing. In fact, in a few days I will be cofacilitating with him in Santa Cruz."

Vicki suggested that Mary call Dan and see what connection they might have with one another that had prompted a summons from a cosmic source.

After a conversation that was pleasant, but didn't provide any meaningful clues, Dan mentioned that his airline tickets had been improperly dated and that he would be flying out three days earlier than was necessary.

"That must be the connection," the psychic told him. "Vicki and I are driving to Mount Shasta to attend a seminar by Mafu. Come with us. It would seem that you are supposed to be at this seminar."

Dan accompanied Vicki and Mary to Mount Shasta, but he became somewhat uneasy when the channeled entity repeated over and over to the audience that they must all open their heart chakras. Dan had survived a nasty divorce, so he was not entirely certain that he wished to open his heart chakra any wider than was absolutely necessary. Not long before, a channeled entity named Solano had told him that his twin flame was on the horizon. As pleasant as that seemed, memories of a shattered marriage had left him in no hurry to be bound to another.

But by the time he left the seminar with Mafu's nearly incessant urging to open the heart chakra, Dan was fired up to maximum heat—and his heart chakra was wide open.

Two days later, he saw *her*—the very same woman he'd seen in a precognitive dream. The one of whom Solano had spoken. She was getting out of a car in the convent parking lot, obviously intending to attend the seminar he was facilitating! *And his heart chakra was wide open.*

Dan felt his knees buckle. Was he having a heart attack? He fell to his knees and was only capable of crawling to the door of the convent.

Amazingly, once the door had closed, blocking his view of *her,* he was able to stand. His heart resumed a normal pace.

Laura's first meeting with Dan was hardly impressive.

"I thought the guy had to be a total jerk," she chuckled at the memory. "He just stood there, trying to shape a coherent sentence. 'H . . . h . . . how are . . . y . . . you?' I thought, *this* is the facilitator? And he can't even make a sentence? What a wonderful weekend this is going to be!"

Dan finally managed to complete the sentence. Laura said she was fine, thank you.

"Then he did it again! 'H . . . how . . . are . . . y . . . y . . . you?' I told him again that I was fine—and I got away as fast as I could to sit beside Vicki on the couch. According to the brochure, Dan Clausing was a hypnotherapist, a channel, a lecturer, a radio personality, and an entrepreneur with a degree in psychology. Terrific! And he couldn't even make small talk.

"Later, Vicki said that from her psychic perspective, what she saw was two enormous balls of energy collide. She said she knew she was watching the reunion of two intimate lovers, and it was so intense that she felt she just wanted to disappear and leave us alone."

That might have been the view from a talented psychic's perspective, but it was just the opposite of what was being enacted on the physical level.

"I had absolutely no attraction to this flustered, stammering, pathetic guy," Laura said.

Later that evening, she found herself alone with Dan, and somehow she could not stand up.

"I didn't want to be alone with him—but there we were."

Laura managed to salvage the awkward moment by giving expression to her talent as a numerologist.

"Pretty soon, I was outlining his life for him. I know I was making solid hits, because his face kept getting redder and redder."

When she discovered that their rooms were opposite one another, she slammed her door in anger, unable to explain her rage.

The next day, during an exercise in an altered state of consciousness, members of the group came back to full wakefulness with stories of having seen Laura together with Dan in past-life love relationships.

"Everyone kept seeing Dan and me in passionate circumstances," Laura said. "I kept wondering what on earth was going on!"

That evening, as she stood alone looking out to sea, Dan approached her and came right out with it. He said that he was having strong feelings toward her. He was falling madly in love with her.

"I thought, 'Spare me, dear Lord!' For ten years on cruise ships I had heard every line in the book. But then I thought, Don't crucify the guy. Be nice."

Laura put on her most professional smile. "Look, please try to understand. I'm not attracted to you. You're just not at all my type. I'm simply not interested in you."

Dan could not be put off. "Laura, I'm forty-five years old, and I've just realized that I have never been in love."

"Don't fall in love with me," she warned him. "Because I feel nothing toward you!"

Laura uttered a prayer that he not try to kiss her, and then she was completely astonished to hear a voice that she eventually recognized as her own saying, "But I could learn to love you."

Had she really said that? She wanted to stuff the words back into her mouth. Where had that come from?

She had to get away from him, and she left him standing there.

When she returned to her room, she saw that Dan had left his door open.

"I became so angry that he would leave his door open, as if inviting me in," Laura said. "And there he was, sitting on his bed, looking like a forlorn little boy. I walked into my room and slammed the door. I told myself that there was no way I was going to go over there!"

But she found herself of two minds: one that didn't want to be with Dan, and another that was beginning to remember, to achieve a deep level of knowing.

It was as if her feet carried her to Dan's room without the consent of her mind and body.

When he looked up, she told him that she would only stay a minute or two to talk. Three hours later, she was still there.

Somehow, although her conscious mind could not believe it, they went to bed together.

"I was not an easy lady," Laura said emphatically. "All those years on the cruise lines had made me immune to the concept of one-night stands. I had been celibate two years just to prove that I was in control.

"When we began to make love, Dan went into terrible convulsions. I had never seen such intense body shakes. He was like a human earthquake, that's the best description I can come up with. I was afraid he was dying. I thought, 'Oh, my God! I've slept with the facilitator and killed him in a nunnery!'"

Laura learned later that the instant their bodies had joined, Dan's physical cells and soul energy had experienced 100 percent remembrance of her and 100 percent knowing that she was his twin flame.

But that night, as soon as she had calmed Dan, she slunk off to her own room, resolved to put an end to things before they really got started.

"The next day, I tried to make it as plain as possible to Dan that he was just not my type," Laura said. "I don't know why I'm even talking to you now," I told him.

As if he had not heard a single one of her protests, Dan asked her to fly back east with him when he facilitated another seminar in New Jersey.

"My brain intended to scream, 'No!'" Laura said, "but the words that came out were, 'Yes, I'll be there.'"

What's happening to me? Laura demanded of the universe.

Dan began to channel for her.

"He started out by calling me 'Beloved Entity' and telling me that I was right on schedule," Laura said. "He said that we had been together in three past lives and that we were twin flames. Coming together in our present lifetime was our reward, so to speak. We were to be teachers to the people and to each other we were to be helpmates and companions through the coming time of transition.

"I thought it was all some act that Dan had come up with to try to manipulate me. I had been in show business and I wasn't about to fall for this gimmick."

When Laura left the seminar, she visited her father in another part of California.

"An old back injury returned with such pain and violence that my father had to take me to the emergency room. As I recuperated in the hospital,

I had lots of time to think, and I realized that symbolically, my back injury was my 'turning my back' on my old ways, my former life.

"Dan called me daily on the telephone, and even though I was brutal and abusive to him, he remained calm and loving."

A week later, Laura was taken to a California airport in a wheelchair to join Dan, who met her with a wheelchair at the New Jersey airport. It had been five weeks since their first meeting in this lifetime.

"I was exhausted from the ordeal, and I was still very confused," Laura said. "Yet I saw nothing but the purest love streaming from Dan's eyes. I made a vow to shut off my intellect, to allow love to enter, to be in my heart and my feelings."

When Laura's full realization came, it arrived with such force that she was temporarily rendered speechless. "I felt intense heat throughout my body as my two opposing selves merged. Immediately, I was madly in love with Dan. Since I had lost my voice, I stated in sign language, 'I love you.' "

Two weeks later, Dan and Laura hiked 14,000 feet up to the snowline on Mount Shasta and spoke their marriage vows to each other.

"The birds were our witnesses," Laura remembered fondly. "Our wedding rings were fashioned from moss. Later, we had an 'official wedding' for members of our families."

Dan and Laura Clausing have now been as one for eight years and state firmly that they still honor their being together.

"Every day we express our gratitude for this

creation. We view our relationship as the distinction for passing through the fires of past lives. We spend twenty-four hours a day together—and it still is not enough. We truly communicate moment to moment. We may have two sentences of frustration between us—and then the very next words between us have no carry-over from the previous emotion. We hold no ill-will. It would seem that our purpose in being together is to be a constant catalyst to the other's growth. We are continually employed through the light of one another."

Author's Note

Many of the people who contributed their own experiences as destined lovers also happen to be men and women who offer their own research, counsel, artistic expression, or inspiration to those who seek more information about the subjects described in *Destined to Love*.

For further details, readers may contact these individuals directly at the addresses listed below:

David and Barbara Jungclaus, Lost World Publishing, 2899 Agoura Road, Suite 381, Westlake Village, California 91361.

Laura and Dan Clausing, Evening Star Ranch, 2376 Egland Road, Addy, Washington 99101.

Tara and Raymond Buckland, P.O. Box 892, Wooster, Ohio 44691-0892.

Patrick and Gael Crystal Flanagan, Vortex Industries, 1109 S. Plaza Way, Suite 399, Flagstaff, Arizona 86001.

Ben Smith, 2929 S.E. Mile Hill Drive, #A-6, Port Orchard, Washington 98366.

Dr. Lawrence Kennedy and Sandra Sitzmann, P. O. Box 611, Kalispell, Montana 59903.

Clarisa Bernhardt, P.O. Box 669, Winnipeg, Manitoba, R3C 2K3, Canada.

Lee Lagé and Stan Kalson, International Holistic Center, 1042 Willow Creek Rd., A111-151, Prescott, Arizona 86301.

Those readers who may wish to share their own stories of destined love or participate in the research of Brad Steiger and Sherry Hansen Steiger may obtain a copy of the **Steiger Questionnaire of Mystical, Paranormal, and UFO Experiences** by sending a stamped, self-addressed business envelope to Timewalker Productions, P.O. Box 434, Forest City, Iowa 50436.

FUN AND LOVE!

THE DUMBEST DUMB BLONDE JOKE BOOK   (889, $4.50)
by Joey West
They say that blondes have more fun . . . but we can all have a hoot
with THE DUMBEST DUMB BLONDE JOKE BOOK. Here's a
hilarious collection of hundreds of dumb blonde jokes — including
dumb blonde GUY jokes — that are certain to send you over the
edge!

THE I HATE MADONNA JOKE BOOK   (798, $4.50)
by Joey West
She's Hollywood's most controversial star. Her raunchy reputation's brought her fame and fortune. Now here is a sensational collection of hilarious material on America's most talked about
MATERIAL GIRL!

LOVE'S LITTLE INSTRUCTION BOOK   (774, $4.99)
by Annie Pigeon
Filled from cover to cover with romantic hints — one for every day
of the year — this delightful book will liven up your life and make
you and your lover smile. Discover these amusing tips for making
your lover happy . . . tips like — ask her mother to dance — have his
car washed — take turns being irrational . . . and many, many
more!

MOM'S LITTLE INSTRUCTION BOOK   (0009, $4.99)
by Annie Pigeon
Mom needs as much help as she can get, what with chaotic sched-
ules, wedding fiascos, Barneymania and all. Now, here comes the
best mother's helper yet. Filled with funny comforting advice for
moms of all ages. What better way to show mother how very much
you love her by giving her a gift guaranteed to make her smile
everyday of the year.

*Available wherever paperbacks are sold, or order direct from the
Publisher. Send cover price plus 50¢ per copy for mailing and han-
dling to Penguin USA, P.O. Box 999, c/o Dept. 17109, Bergen-
field, NJ 07621. Residents of New York and Tennessee must
include sales tax. DO NOT SEND CASH.*

HISTORICAL ROMANCE FROM PINNACLE BOOKS

LOVE'S RAGING TIDE   (381, $4.50)
by Patricia Matthews

Melissa stood on the veranda and looked over the sweeping acres of Great Oaks that had been her family's home for two generations, and her eyes burned with anger and humiliation. Today her home would go beneath the auctioneer's hammer and be lost to her forever. Two men eagerly awaited the auction: Simon Crouse and Luke Devereaux. Both would try to have her, but they would have to contend with the anger and pride of girl turned woman . . .

CASTLE OF DREAMS   (334, $4.50)
by Flora M. Speer

Meredith would never forget the moment she first saw the baron of Afoncaer, with his armor glistening and blue eyes shining honest and true. Though she knew she should hate this Norman intruder, she could only admire the lean strength of his body, the golden hue of his face. And the innocent Welsh maiden realized that she had lost her heart to one she could only call enemy.

LOVE'S DARING DREAM   (372, $4.50)
by Patricia Matthews

Maggie's escape from the poverty of her family's bleak existence gives fire to her dream of happiness in the arms of a true, loving man. But the men she encounters on her tempestuous journey are men of wealth, greed, and lust. To survive in their world she must control her newly awakened desires, as her beautiful body threatens to betray her at every turn.